SO-BZK-246

First impressions . . .

"Tell me about yourself. I have to be able to report something *other* than what I already know."

"Tell me what you know."

She hesitated, but he had made the mistake of asking. "You're a rude, boorish man who eats revolting sausage sandwiches and drinks great quantities of coffee. You also smoke disgusting cigars and scratch your chest with your index finger. Do you suppose that's the kind of information Mrs. Simpson wanted?"

"I doubt it." He continued to inspect her. "Of course, I can tell everyone you're a prissy little lady who eats wilted lettuce and gets nasty when she can't have her own way. You dress only in pastels and wear too much perfume. A professional bleaches your hair."

"That's a lie!"

"How's it going?" Mrs. Simpson approached them, smiling. "Getting a lot of information?"

"Volumes full," Kyle answered her.

Dear Reader,

Although our culture is always changing, the desire to love and be loved is a constant in every woman's heart. Silhouette Romances reflect that desire, sweeping you away with books that will make you laugh and cry, poignant stories that will move you time and time again.

This year we're featuring Romances with a playful twist. Remember those fun-loving heroines who always manage to get themselves into tricky predicaments? You'll enjoy reading about their escapades in Silhouette Romances by Brittany Young, Debbie Macomber, Annette Broadrick and Rita Rainville.

We're also publishing Romances by many of your all-time favorites such as Ginna Gray, Dixie Browning, Laurie Paige and Joan Hohl. Your overwhelming reaction to these authors has served as a touchstone for us, and we're pleased to bring you more books with Silhouette's distinctive medley of charm, wit and—above all—*romance*. I hope you enjoy this book, and the many stories to come.

Sincerely,

Rosalind Noonan
Senior Editor
SILHOUETTE BOOKS

EMILIE RICHARDS
Angel and the Saint

Silhouette Romance

Published by Silhouette Books New York

America's Publisher of Contemporary Romance

To Kathy who brought us Jessie,
and to Jessie who brings us love.

SILHOUETTE BOOKS
300 East 42nd St., New York, N.Y. 10017

Copyright © 1986 by Emilie McGee

All rights reserved, including the right to reproduce
this book or portions thereof in any form whatsoever.
For information address Silhouette Books,
300 East 42nd St., New York, N.Y. 10017

ISBN: 0-373-08429-3

First Silhouette Books printing April 1986

All the characters in this book are fictitious. Any
resemblance to actual persons, living or dead, is purely
coincidental.

SILHOUETTE, SILHOUETTE ROMANCE and colophon are
registered trademarks of the publisher.

America's Publisher of Contemporary Romance

Printed in the U.S.A.

Books by Emilie Richards

Silhouette Romance

Brendan's Song #372
Sweet Georgia Gal #393
Gilding the Lily #401
Sweet Sea Spirit #413
Angel and the Saint #429

EMILIE RICHARDS

grew up in St. Petersburg and attended college in northern Florida. She also fell in love there and married her husband, Michael, who is her opposite in every way. "The only thing we agreed on was that we were very much in love. We haven't changed our minds about that in the sixteen years we've been together." They now live in New Orleans with their four children, who span from toddler to teenager.

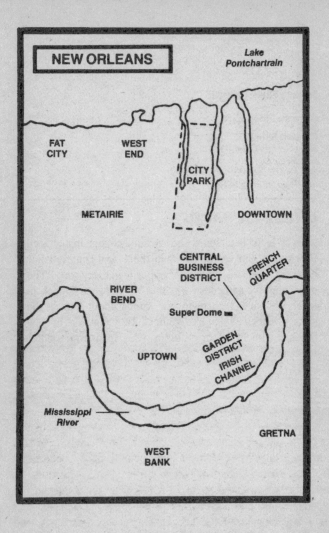

Prologue

Mrs. Simpson was having trouble keeping her eyes open. As a young woman she had been able to make a trip like this one and have energy left over at the end to tend to business. But this time she had traveled for twenty-four hours to get to an infinitesimal speck on the map, and her middle-aged body was telling her it was time to sleep. Only there wasn't time. There were the children. Always the children.

With a yawn, she forced her eyes to remain open as she gazed at the familiar sight of dozens of Oriental cherubs running through the cramped play yard of the orphanage. She had been to this institution once before, and now, as then, she was amazed at the vitality of the black-haired, almond-eyed boys and girls. This was one of the better places for a homeless child to end up. There was love here, and usually enough food. But there wasn't enough room. It was time for some of these children to move on.

Things were changing in Korea. The government was trying to remedy a bad situation, but the job wasn't an easy one. Centuries of tradition dictated against Koreans adopting someone else's children. Fortunately there were couples, thousands of them in countries like the United States, who willingly opened their homes and hearts to those children who couldn't find a place in Korean society. And Kathleen Simpson's job was to see that those matches were made.

A wave from the doorway of the low-slung cement building indicated that the orphanage personnel were ready for her to view the babies they were going to be able to place with Ecumenical Children's Services, the agency Mrs. Simpson headed in far-off New Orleans. With a smile and pats on the head to the children blocking her way, she began moving toward the door and the pleasurable task before her.

But a tiny, forlorn figure caught her attention. Huddled on the sidewalk behind the flying feet of the other children was a little girl about three years old. A single tear perched on the child's nose, but one look was all it took to see that a lifetime of tears lived inside her. The child was the same and yet different from the others clustered in groups in the play yard. The child could not stand.

As Mrs. Simpson watched, a slightly older boy approached the little girl and carefully lifted her to lean against him. And with one practiced gesture, he wiped the tear from her nose with his shirt-sleeve.

Mrs. Simpson watched as the little girl leaned on his shoulder and hobbled with him around the building and out of sight. Adoption work was full of touching moments, but Mrs. Simpson found herself transported by the little boy's simple act of kindness and the aching sadness in the little girl's eyes.

And just as so many important decisions are made with the heart not the head, Kathleen Simpson decided at that instant that she would find homes for those two children herself. Sure, her agency specialized in infants. Sure, families who were looking for older children or handicapped children were sent to other agencies who welcomed their requests. Sure, right now there was no one at home waiting for these children.

None of that mattered. Suddenly Kathleen Simpson felt young again. There were the children. Always the children. Eyes wide open, she marched into the building to begin the process she loved so well.

Chapter One

I will never understand why you won't get married and have children the normal way.''

Angelle Celestine Reed smiled fondly at her grandmother and continued sorting through a rack of ball gowns, fondling the embroidered silks and beaded satins as she went. "Because, Maw Maw, I've never met a man I'd want to marry."

"Sheer and utter nonsense." Marie LaBois, or Maw Maw to her grandchildren, shook her head, temporarily displacing her luxuriant hair, which was tinted a color as blue as the patrician blood that pumped through her Creole veins. "You never give a man a chance."

"That's probably true," Angelle agreed politely.

"Don't think you can get out of this discussion by agreeing with me."

Angelle turned to face the older woman, her small hands still deeply buried in the rich fabrics. "Maw Maw, I really don't want to get married. And I really do want a child. I'm going to adopt one. I start the home-study process tonight. What else can I say?"

"You can say you've changed your mind."

"Not a chance." Angelle turned to the rack of dresses and finished examining them. When she was done, each one of the designer originals was in its proper place, smoothed to fall freely to the floor.

"It's just not done, Angelle. It simply isn't." Madame LaBois rose and stood behind Angelle who had moved to the wall where bridal gowns hung in resplendent display. She watched as Angelle began to tuck plastic coverings over each gown. "I realize that you never had the benefit of a mother to teach you the facts of life, but I thought I had succeeded quite admirably until this latest piece of whimsy. People get married before they have children, Angelle. Before they adopt. Not after."

"I'm twenty-six. If I wait, Maw Maw, I'll die a childless old maid. This way I'll just die an old maid."

"What does Dennis say?"

Angelle grimaced. "He told me last night that if I went through with it, he'd probably never ask me to marry him."

"Well, every cloud has its silver lining."

"Just what I thought." The two women faced each other, and burst out laughing simultaneously. Two generations separated them, but for that brief moment they looked like sisters.

Both were tiny, delicately boned and deceptively fragile in appearance. Angelle's hair, an unearthly silver blond, drifted in a shoulder-length cloud around her face, accentuating huge blue eyes and a nose that could only be called pert. Madame LaBois had the same blue eyes but stronger features that had deepened with age. Tiny lines, foreign to Angelle's flawless skin, marked the older woman's passage through the years.

"I was never sure if Dennis would know how to father a child anyway." Madame LaBois enjoyed the explosive giggle her insult precipitated and then sobered briefly. "But really, Angelle, it might matter to someone else. Someone you could fall in love with."

"If such a man exists, he'll have to take me as I am, Maw Maw. And that means with my daughter, whoever she may be."

With a shrug and a lift of her hands, the older woman gave up the argument. "Well, I don't agree, but I'll love my newest great-grandchild anyway."

It was as close to a blessing as Angelle was likely to get, and she knew it. "Thank you, Maw Maw." She put her arms around her grandmother and gave her a quick squeeze. "And besides, don't you think we need another female in the family?"

"That we do. Those brothers of yours don't seem to have a female chromosome in any of their bulky bodies. Nine great-grandchildren and all of them male." Madame LaBois disappeared into the back room of the expansive shop and returned carrying two purses. She handed one to Angelle. "All finished?"

"I think so." Angelle stepped back and tilted her head to survey the room. Closing up seemed to take longer and longer. When she had taken over the management of LaBois Bridal from her grandmother, the shop had been smaller, catering only to New Orleans' wealthiest citizens. Angelle had expanded the inventory over the two years she had been in charge, adding less expensive ball gowns for the throngs of partygoers who wore them during the carnival season. She had also added more accessories and a complete line of designer dresses for the bride selecting her trousseau. She was thankful that income had soared in direct proportion to the amount of work necessary to keep the shop going, and in addition to Madame LaBois and Angelle, there were several women who helped during their busiest times.

With a final check of the security system that guaranteed she would find the shop in the same condition she left it in, Angelle ushered her grandmother out the front door and secured the final lock.

As always, going from the comfortable air-conditioned temperature of the bridal shop to the high temperature and smothering humidity of a New Orleans August made Angelle gasp for breath. She waved as her grandmother sprinted toward a big Oldsmobile and dived in unceremoniously to start the engine and the car's cooling system.

By the time Angelle had unlocked her own Ford Escort, rolled down the windows and pulled out into the stream of traffic that paraded up and down St. Charles Avenue, her hair was curling in a damp riot around her face. One look in the rearview mirror convinced her that she would not be at her best for her first home-study session.

"Darned air conditioner," she cursed as she stopped at a red light. The accursed air conditioner had stopped working the week before, and Angelle had not had the time to take the car into the shop. Instead she suffered.

Irritably she watched as the light changed. "One thousand one, one thousand two, one thousand three..." She tapped her toe on the gas pedal as she counted the obligatory three seconds before she could pull out into the intersection. She had grown up in New Orleans, and she knew that anyone jumping a green light was as good as dead, just as she knew that no self-respecting New Orleanian would forego the challenge of racing a yellow light.

With reasonable care, she maneuvered the little Escort through the traffic. Luckily she was heading downtown from uptown while everyone else was heading uptown from downtown. Traffic was comparatively light. She would have just enough time to grab a bite at a restaurant near the Ecumenical Children's Services building before the home-study session began.

Ten minutes later she took a ticket from the man in the parking garage next to the ECS building and found a spot to park on the fifth level. High heels clicking briskly on the cement floor, she hurried to the elevator that would take her out to the street.

In the open once more, she investigated the possibilities for a quick dinner. The only viable one seemed to be a seedy little coffee shop advertising po'boy sandwiches and red beans and rice. Since nothing better was in sight, she fought down her distaste and opened the door.

Inside she was greeted by the roar of top forty music from a jukebox and the repeated chatter of a space creature emanating from one of three video games against the side wall. There was a small table in the opposite darkened corner, and she aimed her petite body in its direction, hoping for a certain anonymity in exchange for atmosphere. She reached the table at the same moment that someone else did.

A large man slid into the seat she was claiming for her own a split second before she reached it. Too late to pretend she was going somewhere else, Angelle stopped short of sitting on his lap and pulled herself erect. "Pardon me," she said sweetly, "but that was my seat."

"Now how can that be, little lady? I've been sitting here for at least ten minutes."

Astonished by the bold-faced lie, Angelle drew back and swept the stranger with the coldest stare her wide blue eyes were capable of. "That certainly isn't true," she said as she sized him up. The man was huge. A hulking, sizzling mountain of masculinity. A prizefighter, she decided. Or a wrestler.

Everything about this giant seemed to shout lack of restraint. He was too big. Certainly not fat, not at all. Large. The word "brawny" came to mind immediately. His hair was brown with liberal red highlights, and it curled without restraint all over his head, spilling over his collar. Even his eyebrows were out of control, she thought with disgust. They were wiry and sun bleached, standing up in peaks over outrageous turquoise eyes. His skin was sun darkened and ruddy. An Irishman, she decided. An overgrown leprechaun who probably couldn't tell the truth if he tried.

"You're being too literal," the man corrected her without a smile. "The waiter has already taken my order and I went to the bathroom to wash my hands."

"What a good idea," she said, her polite tone only hinting at sarcasm. Without another word she turned and found her way to a table nearby. The only chair there was turned to face the Irishman's table, and she lowered herself onto it with ladylike finesse. She was absolutely going to love watching the man squirm when the waiter came to take his order.

The Irishman, however, didn't even have the grace to look embarrassed. He was watching her with curiosity and something akin to dislike. His massive body seemed too large for the bentwood chair, and he leaned back, arms clasped behind him. The movement pulled the soft knit of his green polo shirt across the prominent muscles of his barrel chest. The three-button placket was unbuttoned, and lavishly curling chest hair was much in evidence. With a gesture that seemed perfectly natural, he brushed the open placket with his fingertips, scratching his chest with pleasure, as if she weren't sitting right there with her eyes glued to his every movement.

Seemingly satisfied, he banged the chair upright again and reached into his pocket, pulling out a small cigar. With a sly smile and a nod in her direction, he struck a match and lit the cigar, a look of sensuous pleasure stealing over his features. With another nod he blew the smoke directly at her.

It was just what she would have expected. A coarse, rude, man's man, she decided. Large, supremely masculine and uncouth. A man who probably saw himself as God's gift to the female of the species. All in all, he was everything that Angelle didn't like in a man. Absolutely everything.

She refused to react to the cigar smoke. Forcing herself not to blink, she waited patiently for the waiter to arrive to take the Irishman's order. It was only when the harried little man approached the corner table with a gigantic sausage po'boy and a plate of red beans that she realized that she had made a mistake. That realization at almost any other time would have made her feel contrite, sheepish perhaps. But with the Irishman smiling at her and toasting her with his coffee cup, she felt not at all contrite. She felt angry.

Angelle's pert little nose rose two inches in the air as the waiter approached her table and took her order. As she waited for her salad to come, she continued to stare at the man in the corner, watching with disgust as he bit into the dripping sausage sandwich. He ate with obvious relish, strong white teeth tearing into each chunk of sausage and bread, making quick work of a sandwich that would have taken Angelle—who would never have eaten a sausage sandwich anyway—weeks to finish.

Next he polished off the red beans and rice, scooping up the thick residue from his plate with hunk after hunk of French bread. With a sigh, and what Angelle was sure was a belch, the man finished the last of the French bread and settled back in his chair. The temporarily snuffed-out cigar was relit, and once again aimed in Angelle's general direction.

By the time her chef's salad arrived, Angelle had completely lost her appetite. Only the man's insolent stare made her eat the year's supply of lettuce that tasted fully as wilted as it looked.

Kyle Sullivan watched as the pretty little blond finished what looked to be the worst chef's salad in history. God, she was a sweet-looking little morsel. And how he disliked sweet women.

He could still smell the cloud of perfume that had surrounded her as she had stood by his table insisting that he give up his rightful place there. Even his cigar smoke couldn't mask that cloying floral scent. Her high-pitched musical tones still hung in the air too. Like all women of her type, she had expected him to give her what she wanted just because she wanted it. Oh, he had plenty of experience with women like Miss Priss there. And he hadn't enjoyed any of it.

He consulted his watch. He still had time before the home-study session began. He signaled the waiter to bring him another cup of coffee and settled down to watch her some more. It was a lesson, he decided, in what he didn't want in a woman. Not that he really wanted a woman anyway. At age thirty-two, after one abortive attempt at marriage, he was a confirmed bachelor. Still, a man could get caught unawares. It had happened once before, with a woman very much like this one, and he was determined that it would never happen again.

What was it, he asked himself, that set his teeth on edge? She was amazingly pretty, delicate like a piece of Wedgwood porcelain. Her blond hair was startling, almost natural looking with her white skin, although no one had hair that color without help. Her features were regular except for that ridiculous nose, which turned up like a high-school cheerleader's dream. No, there was nothing repugnant about her looks. Nothing that he could put his finger on anyway.

It was the air of pure, overpowering femininity that turned him off. She was dressed in a simple pink sundress with a jacket that matched, and he was certain that under the table were pink high-heeled sandals and a pink purse too. Her makeup was subtle—so subtle, in fact, that he was sure it had taken her an hour to get it exactly right. In short, she was a little lady through and through, and probably a man-hungry, conniving witch to boot.

The vehemence of that last thought temporarily shook him out of his reverie. She was getting up to leave, gliding gracefully across the floor without so much as a glance in his direction. He had been right about the purse and shoes, but the strong prejudice he felt was a surprise. Kyle prided himself on not prejudging others. Still, there was something about that woman... Some other time he'd have to examine those feelings and figure them out, but luckily, he would probably never see this particular female paragon again. If he had prejudices, he'd have to deal with them; he was just glad he wouldn't have to deal with the woman too.

Angelle straightened the skirt of her sundress one last time before she opened the door of the ECS office and ventured inside. The reception room was full of people sitting on straight-backed chairs against the wall. As she had expected, they seemed to be sitting in pairs. Single-parent adoption was relatively new, and Angelle had realized that she might be the only single there. It gave her a twinge of sadness to know that when she went home, there would be no one to share the evening's events with.

There was one empty chair in the corner, and she sat down, smiling tentatively at the couple next to her. Both the husband and wife were middle-aged, and they held hands, beaming like the expectant parents they were. They exchanged pleasantries with Angelle, and she was busily engaged in finding out about them when the door banged shut once again. Looking up to examine the new arrival, Angelle stopped in midsentence. There, standing by the door, was the Irishman.

It couldn't be. This wasn't the corner crap game. This wasn't the ticket office for the local wrestling match. What on earth was he doing here?

Another door opened, and Kathleen Simpson came out of one of the inner offices to greet them. "I see you've all arrived," she stated in a warm voice. "Welcome. I'll show you where the conference room is and where to get coffee if you want it." As one body, everyone in the room rose and followed Mrs. Simpson down the long hall. Angelle couldn't quite believe it, but the Irishman was following too.

She watched his face as he caught sight of her. Her own astonishment was mirrored in his turquoise eyes. With no more sign of recognition than a lifted eyebrow, she brushed past him. I must need a lesson in humility, she decided. What other interpretation could she place on his presence there?

The conference room was spacious and fitted with comfortable armchairs and sofas. Angelle immediately took a chair next to the couple she had met in the waiting room. The Irishman sat as far away as he possibly could. Where was the man's wife, she wondered? Mrs. Simpson had said that everyone was there. Surely she just hadn't noticed that Mrs. Irishman wasn't present yet.

"I'm glad that you're all here," Mrs. Simpson began. "I've talked to each of you individually, so you know what to expect. As I've told you, this home-study process is different from what each of you probably imagined. Originally home studies were conducted individually. An adoption worker would scrutinize you carefully, check dozens of references, examine your financial, social and religious history with a microscope and run her finger over your windowsills to see if you kept a clean house.

"Thank goodness, times have changed. Perfect church attendance and a floor clean enough to eat on are no longer our major criteria for parenthood. I've done a preliminary check of your qualifications. Now it's up to you. This home-study group is going to be helping you make the decision about adoption. If, after our six weeks together are over, you decide that you still want to adopt, we will help you find a child."

Angelle tried to concentrate on the information that Mrs. Simpson was giving them, but her mind and her eyes kept wandering across the room. Why was the Irishman here? Where was his wife? And why did she care?

Finally Mrs. Simpson finished her brief speech. "So," she said with a smile on her pleasant round face, "it's time for you to get to know one another. I'm going to assign each of you a partner and ask you to do a brief interview. At the end of ten minutes, I'll want you to have enough information so that you can introduce your partner to the rest of the group."

Angelle, who was not even faintly psychic, knew beyond the shadow of a doubt who her partner would be. Sure enough, the Irishman had a name. He was Kyle Sullivan, and, of course, he was assigned to her.

When they were settled cozily on one of the sofas with Kyle taking up two-thirds of the space, they finally had to face each other.

"Well," Angelle began. "Fancy meeting you here."

Kyle stretched his long arm on the back of the sofa and took the opportunity to examine her face up close. "Do you mind if I smoke?" he asked after a significant pause.

"Darned right I do," she answered sweetly.

"Funny, I thought maybe you'd feel that way."

The seconds ticked by, and Angelle was increasingly conscious of the hairy, muscled forearm behind her neck. She leaned forward to avoid contact. "Tell me about yourself," she said finally. "I have to be able to report something other than what I already know."

"Tell me what you know."

She hesitated, but he had made the mistake of asking. "You're a rude, boorish man who eats revolting sausage sandwiches and drinks great quantities of coffee. You also smoke disgusting cigars and scratch your chest with your index finger. Do you suppose that's the kind of information Mrs. Simpson wanted?"

"I doubt it." He continued to inspect her. "Of course, I can tell everyone that you're a prissy little lady who eats wilted lettuce and gets nasty when she can't have her own way. You only dress in pastels and wear too much perfume. A professional bleaches your hair."

"That's a lie!"

"You do it yourself? You're quite talented."

"No one does it. It's perfectly natural, and you, Kyle Sullivan, are a—"

"How's it going?" Mrs. Simpson approached them, smiling down at their serious faces. "Getting a lot of information?"

"Volumes full," Kyle answered her.

Kyle and Angelle watched as Mrs. Simpson drifted to the next couple. "We'd better get busy," Angelle said primly. "I'll go first. I'm Angelle Reed." She stopped as Kyle groaned. "What's wrong?"

"Angel? Your name is Angel?"

"Angelle. It's French. I suppose you think I should have been named Gertrude or Patsy."

"Little lady, I couldn't care less. I suppose Angelle suits a sweet young thing. Go on."

"I run a bridal shop." This time she ignored his groans. "In my spare time I design clothes and help with a Campfire troop of six fifth graders."

"I'll bet you take them camping wearing baby pink jeans and high heels."

"Your turn, Mr. Sullivan."

She enjoyed his obvious reluctance to share anything with her. "I own a construction firm," he finally began. "I'm not married, and I'm an ex-football player."

"That figures, although football doesn't seem quite rough enough."

Kyle ignored the interruption. "I've been a Big Brother for four years and I own two golden retrievers that I plan to breed someday."

By Angelle's calculations, they still had five minutes to go. If they sat there not saying anything, they would be very conspicuous, and being conspicuous at an adoption home study was not a good idea at all. "Well, tell me more," she encouraged. "I'm completely fascinated."

"I like tall, athletic females who only wear dresses if they have to. I prefer brunettes to bleached blondes, and I love an earthy, natural woman."

"Funny you should say that," Angelle said, tilting her head to give him the once-over. "I like svelte males who jog. I prefer straight hair to curly, and I love an intelligent, sensitive man."

There were now three minutes hanging in the balance. "I dislike phonies and women who think they can get anything they want," Kyle said smugly.

"I dislike aggressors and men who think they're hotshots."

"I hope you've all gotten the essential information," Mrs. Simpson said, breaking into the buzz of conversation.

"Definitely," Kyle and Angelle said in the same breath.

The introductions seemed to take forever. When it was Kyle's turn to introduce Angelle, he managed to do it politely, if with little enthusiasm. When Angelle stood up and gave Kyle's name, there was an instantaneous burst of applause. "The New Orleans Saint?" a prospective father asked when the noise died down. Angelle turned to see Kyle nodding, his ruddy skin flushed with embarrassment.

Terrific. The man was a celebrity. Having once been a member of New Orleans' own professional football team, Kyle Sullivan was a hero in his hometown. No wonder he was insufferable. Quickly she finished Kyle's introduction. Nothing else she could say mattered. God himself would not have gotten a warmer reception.

The rest of the meeting went by in a haze. Angelle was conscious only of Kyle's arm menacing the back of her neck and his bulky body next to hers. When she noticed everyone else was standing, she stood too, glad that the long session had ended. With marked restraint she did not bolt for the door. Instead she sought out Mrs. Simpson to thank her and tell her goodbye.

"Angelle, can you wait until everyone's gone? I want to talk to you and Kyle alone." Mrs. Simpson waved her back to the sofa where Kyle was still sitting, talking to an admirer.

"She wants to talk to us alone," Angelle told Kyle glumly when his fan left. With care, she perched on the edge of the sofa, hugging the cushioned arm.

"For God's sake, don't look like I'm trying to eat you alive," he snapped at her. "That won't make any kind of impression except a bad one."

He was right. She turned toward him and pretended to look interested in what he was saying. But he wasn't saying anything.

"Kyle, Angelle. Thanks for staying." Kathleen Simpson pulled a chair in front of them. "I just wanted to tell you both that I'm delighted to have you in the group. You're the first single people that this agency has worked with, and we handpicked you both. You're sort of our test cases. As such, I'm going to have to scrutinize you a little more carefully than I will some of the other people here, but I'm sure you'll both measure up just fine."

"Scrutinize?" Angelle asked.

"I'll be talking to friends and neighbors, relatives, business associates. I want to be sure that you can handle the stress of single parenthood."

"It's too bad that everyone in the world who wants a child doesn't have to go through this kind of process," Kyle said.

"If they did," Mrs. Simpson said with a smile, "there probably wouldn't be any children to adopt." She hesitated as if trying to decide whether to share something else with them. "I also think I should tell you that I've got a child in mind for each of you. I'll tell you more when the time comes."

It was only when she and Kyle were outside the office in the corridor that Angelle realized they were alone. Everyone else had gone on ahead of them. Without a word, she marched to the elevator and punched the button. When it arrived she stepped inside, followed closely by Kyle.

"Didn't your mother ever tell you that you shouldn't get into an elevator with a strange man?" he chided her, moving closer as the elderly elevator began its slow descent from the eighth floor to the first.

"I don't think my mother would have suspected that a man as strange as you even existed," she answered, inching closer to the door. The light above her head assured her that they had moved. They were now on the seventh floor.

"You hear such awful stories," he said softly. "The supermarket tabloids are full of them. 'Young Woman Trapped in Elevator with Creature from Outer Space.' 'Young Woman Mysteriously Disappears Between—'" he checked the lights over their head "'—the Fifth and Sixth Floors.'"

"How about, 'Disgusting Maniac Found Mangled by Spike Heel in Elevator.'" She turned to face him as she delivered her headline, only to discover that he was almost on top of her. Before she could protest, the elevator screeched and came to a momentary pause somewhere close to the fourth floor.

"I can't imagine anything worse happening to me than being stuck in this elevator with you," Angelle said through clenched teeth.

Kyle bared his own teeth. "'Man Stays Surprisingly Healthy in Forgotten Elevator. Bones of Woman Found Beside Him.'"

The elevator started again with a jolt, and Angelle was pitched forward, directly at Kyle. In a fraction of a second, he was steadying her against him, arms wrapped closely around her. "Well," he said thoughtfully, "how about, 'Little Lady Finds a Real Man in World's Slowest Elevator.'" And then with a response to the situation that surprised them both, his mouth came down on hers.

There was no sense in struggling. Instinctively Angelle knew that Kyle had no intention of hurting her—he was probably trying to make her angry. It was just one more in a long series of put-downs, and Angelle was determined to treat it just that way. At least that's how she tried to treat it.

But Kyle's mouth was warm on hers, and the hard muscular body that she had found so repugnant felt surprisingly good. Was it the slow motion of the elevator that was causing her head to feel woozy and her feet to lose their grip on the firm floor beneath them? Something that had started out as another insult was fast getting out of hand, at least for her. When she pulled her mouth indignantly away from Kyle's, the look on his face convinced her that his reaction was similar.

"So that's where all the sparks have been coming from," he said finally. They had progressed to the second floor.

"I am not attracted to you. Not the least little bit," she said, outraged at the truth. "You are everything I don't like in a man."

"And you, Angel, are everything I don't like in a woman."

"At least we agree on something," she said.

For the first time, Kyle's tone was not sarcastic. "I think, Angel, that we might agree on more than you can imagine. And I for one don't intend to find out how much more."

The elevator doors opened, and with a faint nod Kyle stepped off and disappeared down the hall. It was only after the elevator doors began to close again that Angelle realized she hadn't gotten off herself.

Chapter Two

Angelle stopped the elevator on the second floor and got off to find the stairs. By the time she reached the parking garage and took that elevator to the fifth level, she was fairly sure that Kyle was long gone. With her luck, his car had probably been parked next to hers. Actually, she decided as she walked to the little Ford Escort, Kyle Sullivan probably didn't drive a car. Most likely he drove a pickup truck. Or a tank.

Still, she found herself peering out of the corner of her eye at any suspicious movement. She was always suspicious in dark, empty garages; a woman couldn't be too careful. Tonight, however, it was more than that. She really was expecting Kyle to pop up out of nowhere. She couldn't seem to shake off his lingering malicious presence.

Her car looked like a haven of security as she unlocked it, scrambling behind the wheel to relock the door behind her. Safely inside, she smiled to herself, glad that she was finally going to be able to go home and forget about the outrageous New Orleans Saint. The engine started with a pleasant whir, and she flung her arm over the seat, turning her head as she put the car in reverse. The car wouldn't move.

Maybe she didn't have it in gear. She shifted again to be sure. She pressed the gas pedal. The car still wouldn't move.

Was the emergency brake on? No. Was there anything else she could check inside? No. She turned off the engine and beat her fists helplessly on the steering wheel. Then, regaining her lost composure, she unlocked the door and got out to investigate.

Each parking space was defined by a heavy metal chain that was strung in front of the spot where the cars' bumpers came to rest. When Angelle had parked originally, the chain had been lax, but as she could see now, after she had left her car, two more cars had parked beside her, pushing against the chain and hooking it firmly under her fender. At that moment, the Ford Escort resembled nothing more than a trinket on an enormous charm bracelet.

The alternatives were few. She could go downstairs to the parking attendant and report her problem, but help from that quarter seemed unlikely. In fact, unless the attendant turned down the huge radio he had been listening to when she had passed him before, there was no chance he'd even hear her complaint.

She could wait until the other cars were moved, freeing her, but that could take hours. As close as the garage was to the French Quarter and the questionable attractions of Bourbon Street, she might have to wait until dawn.

The last alternative was to try to solve the problem herself, holding out hope that she could call one of her brothers to come give her assistance if it became absolutely necessary. "No wonder they're always trying to marry me off," she muttered as she got back in the car.

She had noticed that there were inches to spare before she scraped the cement wall in front of her. Hoping that moving the car in that direction would loosen the chain, Angelle carefully inched it forward until she was almost touching the wall. Getting out once more, she knelt beside the car, her bottom sticking high in the air, to see if her maneuvers had done any good.

The roar of a motor from the ramp behind her had barely penetrated her consciousness when there was a loud revving of an engine and then a sudden cessation of sound. A huge motorcycle of the Hell's Angels variety had pulled into the empty space behind Angelle. Aware that her sundress was lifting with the air current caused by the motorcycle's arrival, Angelle pulled her dress down and as gracefully as she could manage, got up from the cement floor.

"There I was, just driving down the ramp, and what do I see sticking up, practically in my face? The sweetest little fanny this side of the Mississ—"

"Kyle Sullivan!" Angelle cut him off sharply. "You can just be on your way. I don't need you." But she did, and that fact was painfully evident to both of them.

"It seems you're in a bit of a fix, Angel. I might be persuaded to help, if you ask nice." Kyle pulled off his helmet and goggles and strode over to the Escort, resting one foot on her front fender. With careless strength, he jiggled the car up and down easily. The movement tightened the soft knit of his slacks around the bulging muscles of his thighs.

Angelle looked away, telling herself that such blatant masculinity was nauseating. "When I ask you for a favor, Kyle Sullivan, hell will be the site of the next winter Olympics."

She stood there in her spike heels and her pink sundress, now grimy around the hem, watching as he shrugged and took his foot off the fender. He leaned against the hood, arms folded across his big chest. "I'm waiting."

The situation was impossible. She peeked at her watch. It was well past ten o'clock, and she was feeling the effects of a long day. She could call her brother Charles, but Charles would be asleep by now. Her brother John was probably working late, and brother Michael lived in far-off Kenner. She could try Dennis, her occasional boyfriend, but Dennis would have even less idea how to get out of this fix than she did.

"The night's not getting any younger, Angel."

"Will you please help me get my car off that chain?" she finally asked in a strangled tone.

"Ah, I can hear the little demons dusting off their ice skates. You did that well, Angel. Such a perfect little lady."

She was sure that there was steam coming out of her ears. She wanted nothing more than to use his bulky body as a punching bag. Instead, she smiled sweetly. "How lovely that you're capable of recognizing good manners when you see them. There's hope for you, Mr. Sullivan."

She was surprised when he smiled at her retort. She had to admit it. Kyle Sullivan had a smile that could stop traffic. With those big, strong white teeth lined up evenly, peeking out from that roguish mouth, he was something to behold.

"Well, little lady. Let's have a look at it." He was down on the ground in a second, peering underneath the bumper. "How'd you manage this, Angel? I've never seen anything so hopelessly stuck in my life."

She refused to defend herself, waiting until he surfaced. "Can you do anything about it?" she asked him when he was standing again.

"I'm going to bounce on the bumper and try to jiggle it loose. You put what little there is of you on that chain and hold it down as tightly as you can. We'll see if that helps."

With his considerable strength, Kyle was able to move the car up and down, and with Angelle's pressure on the chain itself, the chain began to slide away from the groove beneath the bumper that was holding it so securely.

"Get in and move it up another inch or so and I think we'll have it," Kyle said, waving his hand at the driver's seat, his head under the front bumper again.

"But I'll scrape the front fender."

"Angel, move the car."

Kyle pulled his head out of the way and she inched the car forward until she had bumped the wall. "Better?" she asked acidly. "Or do you want me to keep going right through the cement?"

"Terrific idea," he mumbled, his head under the bumper again.

When he was erect once more, she got out to stand beside him. "Well?"

"I'm going to jump on it with everything I've got. You hold that chain down and it should pop right out."

"But the fender's going to scra—" The sound of metal grinding against cement assaulted her ears, followed by the ping of the chain popping out from under the bumper.

To his credit, Kyle looked embarrassed. "Well, you're free now," he said turning up his hands in a little-boy gesture.

"If that's not just like a man," Angelle exploded. "If you had just stopped to listen to me, I could have told you that would happen, but no, would you listen? Not a chance..."

"The car drifted a fraction of an inch when I jumped on the bumper. If you'd put on the emergency brake, it wouldn't have scraped. If you'd been careful, you wouldn't have gotten yourself into that predicament anyhow. Besides..."

"And if you hadn't come along, I'd have called someone who knew what they were doing and..."

"If I hadn't come along, you'd still be standing here wringing your delicate little..."

"You are insufferable. A true credit to your sex!"

"And you, little lady, are a simpering Barbie doll!

"Male chauvinist!"

"Pigheaded female!"

Simultaneously they pounced on the seats of their vehicles and started their engines. Sure that if she backed out first, Kyle would pile right into her, Angelle waited until he had roared away. Then carefully—boiling beneath her surface control—she backed out of the parking space and followed the exhaust fumes of Kyle's big cycle down the ramp.

The final straw to a very trying day occurred when she discovered that the time she had taken to untangle her car from the chain was going to cost her an extra dollar.

Angelle had spent twenty-six years living in New Orleans. And to her knowledge, she had never once, in all those years, set eyes on Kyle Sullivan. But after the first session of the home study, Kyle Sullivan was everywhere.

"There has to be more than one red-and-silver Yamaha in the city," she told herself the next day when she stopped by the small neighborhood grocery store where she did her shopping. Parked in the lot was a duplicate of Kyle's motorcycle. She pulled her Ford Escort with its permanently scratched bumper in beside the Yamaha and examined the powerful FJ 1100 suspiciously before getting out.

The bike looked the same, but then what did she know? She refused to be paranoid, and she wasn't about to change her shopping habits on such flimsy evidence. By the time she had gone down several aisles and hadn't seen Kyle, she had almost forgotten.

Almost forgotten, that is, until her cart was bumped from the front as she was kneeling down, baby blue skirts swirling gracefully around her knees, inspecting the prices on large sacks of cat food.

"Excuse me," a deep voice said, and when she looked up to smile and say that it was perfectly all right, it was to find Kyle Sullivan glaring at her.

"What are you trying to damage this time, Mr. Sullivan? My shopping cart?" she asked in dulcet tones. "You'll be disappointed to find that it really belongs to the store, not to me."

"You're going the wrong way."

"Oh, really? I didn't notice that the store had put up one-way signs in the aisles. Show them to me." She flashed him a pearly white smile, sucking in her cheeks to be sure that he noticed her dimples at the same time. Instinctively, she knew that dimples would be her ultimate weapon.

He blanched, and she was sure he probably wanted to gag at the outrageous display of femininity. "Everyone else in this store is following a prevailing traffic pattern. Everyone except you."

She fluttered her eyelashes and watched as he turned even whiter. "If a man does not keep pace with his companions, perhaps it is because he hears a different drummer," she quoted sweetly.

"It takes two to speak the truth—one to speak, and another to hear," he responded.

"Congratulations," she said with genuine surprise. "You've read Thoreau too. I didn't know that Classic Comics had condensed *Walden* or *A Week on the Concord and Merrimack*."

"Has it ever occurred to you, Angel, to be careful of that sharp little tongue?" Kyle bent over and lifted her with no apparent strain, one hand firmly cupped beneath her bent elbow. He leaned over until his face was a scant inch from hers. "If you're not careful, I'll put it to better use."

It was her turn to blanch. "You wouldn't dare," she whispered. She was uncontrollably aware of his hulking masculinity so close to her fragile femininity. "Remember,

I represent everything you hate in the female of the species."

"I'm not having any trouble remembering that, little lady. You're making that very easy." He stepped back and gave her a slow perusal. "However, I might enjoy teaching you that there's more to life than prissy manners and baby doll mannerisms."

She stared at him without blinking. "Careful there, big boy. Underneath this cotton candy exterior exists a woman who could give you a run for your money. Care to take a chance?" With a tremendous display of coordination she managed to flutter her eyelashes, flash her dimples and wiggle her hips, all at the same time.

With a look of utter disgust, Kyle saluted her and started down the aisle. In the wrong direction.

The next time Angelle saw Kyle was even more of a surprise.

Several nights after the grocery store incident, Angelle came home from work, fixed herself and her cat, Miaou, an early supper and straightened her side of the little shotgun house.

The house was hers, purchased by her oldest brother, Charles, well before owning a shotgun house had become a status symbol. Her brother, a successful realtor, had sold it to Angelle at a small profit when he'd decided to move into a modest little eighteen-room mansion in the historic Garden District near LaBois Bridal. Angelle's house was a double, each side exactly the same as the other, and she rented the opposite side to a young couple for extra income.

The house was laid out one spacious room behind another with no hallway, in order to conserve square footage. Supposedly one could fire a shotgun from the front porch through to the backyard without hitting a thing, hence the name. The no-nonsense room arrangements made cleaning the house a simple matter, and Angelle had done the necessary chores in a few minutes.

It was a humid evening, but a refreshingly cool breeze was blowing, and it seemed like a shame to waste nature's own air conditioning. Angelle stripped off the mint green skirt and blouse that she had worn all day and changed into white terry-cloth shorts and a lavender polka-dotted tank top.

"Come on, Miaou," she called to the big Persian ball of fluff. "Let's go to the park."

Angelle snapped a leash on to the cat's collar, and then picked up Miaou, burying her face momentarily in the long white fur. "If you're good, I'll let you chase the ducks. Only don't forget you're not allowed to catch them."

Audubon Park, one of two extensive parks within the New Orleans city limits, was a short walk from Angelle's house. She lifted her hand to her neighbors who were sitting outside on their front porches, enjoying the cool air. New Orleans was a city with a city's unique problems, but many neighborhoods still retained a family feeling. Angelle knew that if she ever needed assistance, some of those friendly faces would be there before she could shout for help. It was a comforting thought, and it had helped her make the decision to try to adopt a child.

The park was alive with joggers, cyclists and mothers and fathers with their children. Careful to stay clear of people walking big dogs, Angelle headed for the shore of one of the little lagoons, Miaou in tow. The park was so large that it was still possible, even with all the people there, to find a quiet spot to be alone.

Set free, Miaou began to daintily explore the tall weeds at the lagoon's edge. Angelle sat on the grass, knees pulled up under her chin, watching the cat sneak up on ants and earthworms.

There was children's laughter in the background, and Angelle fantasized about her own daughter-to-be.

The little girl was alive somewhere at that very moment. Angelle knew this was true because she had asked to be given an older child. In fact, she suspected that she was having her home study done now because of that request. Not everyone wanted a child who already had a history.

Mrs. Simpson had mentioned a particular child. What would she be like? Where would she come from? Curly hair or straight, she wondered. Brown eyes or blue? Angelle had specified a child aged three to eight. She suspected she would be given a younger child because of her own relative youth. "I'll be a good mother," she told Miaou, who was stalking a minnow swimming at the edge of the water. "I'll make up for whatever has happened to her, but I won't pity her. It will take time, but she'll be mine in every way."

Somehow, it seemed like a shame that she only had a cat to share such important feelings with.

Miaou was lifting one delicate paw to bat at the minnow when a rough shout alerted both the cat and her owner to approaching danger. Angelle looked up to see two huge golden retrievers bearing down on the little animal. She lunged at the white ball of fur, trying to shield Miaou with her own body, but the cat had taken matters into her own paws. Forced to choose between two terrifying, slobbering canine giants and an endless body of water, the cat had chosen the water. With a dive that would have made a sea lion proud, Miaou was in the lagoon, swimming for all she was worth. The dogs had reached the water's edge, but a signal from their owner stopped them from going after the cat. Instead they began to bark ensuring that Miaou would swim even farther away from shore.

"Cats can't swim," Angelle said, hysteria encroaching.

"That one sure can." Kyle Sullivan stood beside her, a hand on the collar of each of the two retrievers.

"Do something," Angelle wailed. "She'll drown." She turned to plead with the man beside her until she saw who he was. Her hysteria was swapped for pure, unadulterated rage. "I should have known they were your dogs." Without another word, Angelle kicked off her high-heeled sandals and waded into the water after the cat.

"Don't get your feet wet, little lady. You might melt." With a whistle and a shouted command, Kyle took his hand off the collar of one of the dogs, and the dog jumped into the water with a loud splash, drenching Angelle as he swam quickly after the cat. In a moment, dog and cat were safely on shore. Angelle followed closely behind.

"Drop her, Knute." Obediently the retriever opened his magnificent jaws, and the spitting feline was deposited at Angelle's feet.

Angelle grabbed the cat, receiving deep scratches in the process, and hoisted her to rest against the polka-dot tank top. "What do I say?" she asked, turning to Kyle. "Do I say thank you for rescuing Miaou, or do I call you every name I can think of for letting those two monsters loose in the first place?"

"Profuse thank-yous would certainly be out of character. And you've already called me every name you could possibly think of. How about just admitting that bringing a cat to the park is a harebrained idea at best." He looked closely at Miaou. "That is a cat, isn't it?"

Miaou was in sad shape after her ordeal. Her fluffy white fur was matted and brown from the muddy water. Even to Angelle, the cat was unappealing. The retrievers, on the other hand, were sleek and healthy looking; Knute, the rescuer, had shaken off the lagoon water and was drying to a deep reddish gold.

Angelle glared at Kyle, unable to think of a retort nasty enough, but Kyle was paying no attention to her. He was gazing closely at the cat, and where the cat was resting.

"It's a funny thing," he murmured. "Sometimes things turn out in the darnedest ways."

"What are you talking about?" she snapped.

He continued to stare at the cat. "Who would have thought that just taking a simple walk today I'd get to see so much of the little lady's body?"

She looked down and saw that the retriever's splash and Miaou's sodden fur had completely drenched the tank top, leaving the curves of her small breasts plainly visible. Since she hadn't felt it was necessary to wear a bra under the tank top, every detail of her slender body was fast becoming evident.

"Take a good look, Kyle Sullivan, and memorize what you see," she answered, tilting her nose in the air. "I doubt that the likes of you will ever have a chance to see a lady's body again." With a flounce of her terry-cloth-covered hips, she turned and sauntered slowly out of the park. The yapping of the retrievers didn't quite cover up the sound of Kyle's laughter.

"So he keeps popping up." Angelle was relating the story of Kyle Sullivan to her grandmother. Wednesday night had arrived again, and Angelle was closing LaBois Bridal in preparation for the second home-study session.

Madame LaBois lifted one perfect eyebrow. "He sounds fascinating. And of course I've heard of him."

"You have?" Angelle was surprised, although she shouldn't have been. Madame LaBois was something of a New Orleans trivia buff, with a collection of facts about almost everything at her fingertips.

"Yes, darling. And if you'd been paying attention, you'd have heard of him too."

"I hate football, and I despise football players. Even—" Angelle pretended to gasp for air "—the New Orleans Saints."

"I wasn't talking about football, darling. Although, of course I know about Kyle Sullivan's career. No, I was talking about the wedding register."

"The wedding register?" In addition to clothing female members of the wedding party, Angelle sometimes acted as a wedding consultant, keeping track of the facts and figures of elaborate weddings that needed a professional in addition to the mothers and aunts who really ran the show. Wedding preparations that were now in progress were kept in a special wedding register at LaBois Bridal. Every detail of impending celebrations was entered in the book.

"Look on page ninety-four of our newest volume. The Riley wedding, to be held in the City Park rose garden, I do believe."

Angelle pulled the heavy volume down and scanned the appropriate page. With a sinking heart she discovered that Kyle Sullivan was to be Clayton Riley's best man. And she had committed herself to working closely with the preparations for this wedding because the bride's mother lived out of town and could only come the day of the ceremony. "Terrific," she said, slamming the volume shut. "Just terrific!"

"You'd make a lovely couple," her grandmother purred. "He's so big, so masculine, and you're so tiny and feminine."

"He's big, all right. A big jerk."

"All that animosity isn't like you, Angelle. Has the man made a pass at you?"

Angelle, who had neglected to relate the story of the elevator kiss, shook her head. "No—what a revolting idea."

"Darling, I've seen Kyle Sullivan in person. There's nothing revolting about the man. He's absolutely gorgeous."

"If you like solid muscle all over, including between the ears!"

"Did you know that he graduated from Tulane with honors? And that he was on his way to law school when he was drafted by the Saints?"

"Where do you come up with these statistics, Maw Maw?"

"I, for one, am not oblivious to a hunk, darling."

Angelle stared at her grandmother. "And I am?"

"Totally blinded. Every real man who's come your way since you were fifteen has been turned down flat as a crepe. Tell me, Angelle. What do you have against virility?"

Angelle sank onto the arm of one of the comfortable chairs in the corner of the shop and continued to stare at Madame LaBois. "This is a very strange conversation to be having with one's grandmother."

"But then, I've always been a rather strange grandmother."

"You've been the only person in my life who's made sense, Maw Maw."

Madame LaBois settled herself on the chair next to Angelle. "Your father and your brothers worship the ground you walk on. They raised you the best way they knew how."

Angelle nodded. "They're wonderful. All of them, and I adore them. But you were the only person in all those years I was growing up who let me be a girl. To them, I was just another boy."

"Little A.C. in her hand-me-down blue jeans and her baseball caps," Madame LaBois reminisced.

"The only dresses I owned were the ones you bought me."

Her grandmother nodded, "And I remember having to twist your father's arm to make him stop taking you to the barber shop with your brothers."

"What would I have done without you? This was the only place in my little world where anyone paid any attention to who I really was." Angelle smiled a suspiciously tearful smile. "But what does all this have to do with Kyle Sullivan?"

"Have you ever thought it might just be time to stop reacting to everything masculine in the world? You were swallowed up by men as a child, but you're not a child anymore. You can hold your own now." Madame LaBois stood and straightened her skirt. "Anyhow, it's something to think about." She bent over and kissed Angelle on the forehead. "I hope the home study goes well tonight." With a wave, she was gone.

If Angelle hadn't known better, she would have believed that Mrs. Simpson and Maw Maw were in cahoots. Settled comfortably in an armchair on the other side of the room from Kyle Sullivan, Angelle listened to Mrs. Simpson explain the concept of parent tapes.

Parent tapes, it turned out, were not recordings of Dr. Seuss stories that Mom and Dad gave as Christmas presents. They were messages implanted in each child's brain by Mom and Dad and other authorities. They were implanted very early in life, and they became the "shoulds" of everyday living.

Balancing these parent tapes were feelings, emotions, instincts that comprised the "child" part of each person. And the "adult" part, or the rational, well-thought-out part, was the final portion that went into making each human being unique.

"Understanding yourself is an important part of being a parent," Mrs. Simpson finished. "You have to understand yourself to become more than you already are. If you find yourself reacting strongly to something or someone, it's helpful to know why."

Angelle slid lower in her seat. She knew that if she looked in Kyle Sullivan's direction, his eyes would be cemented on her.

"I'm going to pass out some questions now. I want you to answer them, and then I'm going to give you time with your spouse to go over your answers. Kyle, Angelle, will you come here a minute?"

Angelle smoothed her buttercup dress and slipped her gold sandals back on. She stood meekly in front of Mrs. Simpson. "I'd like the two of you to be partners when we divide into duos like this. You both seem open enough to be able to share these rather personal questions. Will that be all right?"

No matter how nonjudgmental Angelle knew Mrs. Simpson to be, she couldn't face telling her that she really didn't even want to sit next to Kyle, much less share anything with him. She nodded glumly. "Certainly." Kyle echoed her answer.

Angelle took her questions back to her chair and barely controlled an agonized groan. The questions were personal. Very personal. Usually she didn't mind talking about her feelings with anyone.... But Kyle Sullivan?

Thirty minutes later, the room was beginning to buzz with shared dialogues. When Angelle looked up, she saw that Kyle had been waiting impatiently for her to finish. She slipped her sandals on again and walked to the empty chair beside him. In the past two hours she had given her reaction to Kyle Sullivan a lot of thought. She was an adult, and she operated on an adult level most of the time. She should be able to control her feelings about this big, hulking, insensitive Irishman.

"Well," she said in an even tone. "Together again." Was it a nervous habit, or was Kyle Sullivan unbuttoning the top three buttons of his shirt just to annoy her. She pressed grimly onward. "Would you like to go first?"

"Little ladies first," he said, flashing his big white teeth at her.

She couldn't; she just couldn't share anything with him. He was impossible, a swine, a throwback to the caveman. And she was just about to tell him so when she noticed Kathleen Simpson walking by. "Well," Angelle began, "I made a list of everything that I like about myself." She picked up the pages covered with her flowery script and began to read. "I'm very organized. I'm polite. I never forget a birthday. I go to church every Sunday. I try to be kind—" she challenged his choking laughter with a glare "—at least most of the time, and I genuinely care about the future of the human race."

"That's all?"

"I bet your list wouldn't fit on a roll of toilet paper," she snapped. "I'll bet there's not enough ink in New Orleans to write all the good things you think about yourself."

Kyle picked up his list. Angelle was appalled by her glimpse of his sprawling, unreadable script. "I'm generous..."

"With insults," she muttered.

"Fun to be with, I have a sense of humor that doesn't quit, I'm good-looking, strong and concerned. I'm loyal, careful, aware of my own powers and..."

"Conceited?" she supplied.

"Well adjusted," he finished.

There was a long pause. Mrs. Simpson walked by again, staring at them curiously. "These are the things I don't like about myself," Angelle ground out. "I have a quick temper, I tend to see things from one side only, and there are certain parts of myself I'm not fully in touch with." She paused as she thought of her grandmother's words. "I don't try new things often enough, and I'm too outspoken." She was sure that all the color had drained from her face.

When she finally peeked at Kyle, she was surprised to see the look of admiration there. "Well, Angel," he said. "That was well done." He picked up his list and cleared his throat.

"I have a rotten temper, I forget that life has two sides to it, I am not always aware of why I act the way I do." He looked up at her and grinned. "Does any of this sound familiar?"

She nodded, surprised.

Kyle continued. "I get stuck on the same old things, and I don't control my tongue very well."

They stared at each other, amazed at their similarities. How could two people who were complete opposites have so much in common?

Neither of them noticed that everyone else was standing. "Thank you for coming," Mrs. Simpson said, breaking into the buzz of friendly conversation. "I'll look forward to seeing you next Wednesday. I hope that all of you learned something tonight."

Kyle and Angelle remained seated, their eyes locked on each other.

Chapter Three

Mrs. Simpson was in the hallway saying goodbye to the last of the prospective adoptive couples when Kyle and Angelle finally stood and prepared to leave. After they said their goodbyes to her, Angelle followed Kyle's path to the elevator.

"Are you sure you want to get in this elevator with me again, Angel?" he asked finally, breaking the long silence between them.

"Only if you promise not to recite any more of your good points," she answered. But real sarcasm was lacking. Both of them were still thinking about the home-study session.

The elevator doors closed behind them, and side by side, they leaned against the railing as the elevator began its slow descent.

"You know, Angel, Mrs. Simpson is no fool," Kyle said as they reached the sixth floor. "She's bound to notice the—" he searched for a word "—animosity, shall we say, between us."

"I've thought of that. I'm trying to be tolerant, Kyle. I really am." Angelle couldn't believe it. She and Kyle Sullivan were having a conversation. A real conversation like two normal people.

"I'm trying too, Angel. Believe it or not, I've been attempting to behave as civilly as I possibly can."

Angelle choked back the words that rose in her throat. She wouldn't. She simply wouldn't be the one to break the spell. "Well," she said after she was in control again, "with both of us trying so hard, I'm sure everything will turn out fine."

"I'm not so sure. Even with both of us trying so hard, there's still a lot of hostility in the air."

"And?"

"And I think we need to sit down and discuss it."

"Aren't you afraid that if we sit down together any more than we have to that things will get worse, not better?" Angelle turned to monitor his expression.

"That's a chance we'll have to take. I don't want anything to jeopardize this adoption." Kyle turned to face her. "Why don't we go have a drink together and clear the air? Mrs. Simpson is right. When people react so strongly to each other, there has to be a reason."

"We're only on the third floor; we probably have time to tell each other every minute detail of our past lives before this elevator gets to the lobby."

"You're avoiding the issue, Angel."

Angelle sighed. "I really don't think—"

He interrupted. "Besides, I'd be interested in finding out why you've been following me this week."

She inhaled sharply and let out a roar. "Following you, you big Irish oaf! I haven't been following you. Where do you get off accusing me of—"

"See? We have a lot to straighten out, don't we? But then, if you're afraid to spend the evening with me..."

"Where shall I meet you?" she said, fire in her eyes. "Just name a place."

"Molly's Irish Pub."

She shook her head. "The Levee Lounge at the Marriott," she suggested.

"Pat O'Brien's."

"The Sazerac at the Fairmont," she countered.

"Bart's Lighthouse Inn on Lakeshore Drive."

"Done," Angelle agreed as the elevator doors opened. "When?"

"Half an hour." He turned and walked away. "And don't forget to get off the elevator this time," he reminded her when he reached the end of the corridor.

Angelle arrived at Bart's before Kyle. It was a warm evening, just perfect for sitting outside on the long wooden deck that overlooked Lake Ponchartrain. She settled herself at a small table and let the lake breeze attempt to cool her shattered composure. There were sailboats docked at the water's edge, and she watched them with interest.

"Have you ordered anything yet?" Kyle slid onto a chair across from her.

She shook her head, unwilling to break the spell the cooling night air was weaving around her.

"I'll have whiskey and water," Kyle told the attractive young waitress who appeared at their table. "Angelle?"

"A Ramos gin fizz," she said.

The young girl was gone for long minutes and back to present them with their drinks before either of them said another word.

"Is calling me by my rightful name a signal of some new and serious attempt to have a conversation?" Angelle finally began.

"It was a mere slip of the tongue," Kyle corrected her. "But if it will help, I'll do it again. Angelle—that's a curious name. How did you come by a French first name with a last name like Reed?''

"Creole blood on my mother's side.''

He nodded. "Old New Orleans family.''

"Actually, old New Orleans on both sides. My father's family came here with the first wave of Americans and settled in the Garden District. My mother's family traces their roots from one of the young girls sent to Louisiana as brides by King Louis, but then everyone in New Orleans does.''

"Not everyone. My people came over from Ireland after the Louisiana Purchase and started an importing business. Old New Orleans again, and not a drop of French blood anywhere.''

"Touché.''

They sat quietly finishing their drinks. Kyle signaled for another round. "So tell me, why do I keep running into you now.''

"Where do you live?''

"Uptown, on Henry Clay.''

"I live on Calhoun. Evidently we're neighbors.''

The thought was depressing to both of them. "We could set up alternate nights at the park,'' Kyle said finally. "I could do my grocery shopping on Wednesdays and Saturdays and you could do yours on Tuesdays and Fridays.''

"You could give me your phone number, and I could call before going anywhere to make sure we don't run into each other.''

"I could move to Oregon.''

"There's a thought.''

They finished their drinks, and Kyle signaled for another round. "How well do you tolerate liquor?'' he asked as the waitress came to the table.

"Well enough, but make this one a soft drink.''

"Two Cokes,'' he ordered.

"So tell me why you want to adopt a child." Kyle was leaning back in his seat, hands behind him encircling his chair. The movement pulled his navy blue dress shirt tighter around his chest, and Angelle, who was feeling very relaxed, actually found herself admiring his physique.

"I love kids," she said with a smile. She leaned back too, with unconscious feminine grace, and shook her cloud of silvery hair back from her face. "I always have. It's not popular to have big families, but I'd like nothing better than to have a bunch of little ones. And after a lot of thought, I decided that I wasn't getting any younger. Now is the time to start my family."

"Why adoption?"

"I'm not married, so it seemed like the only moral alternative." She smiled at Kyle's laughter. "Really though, I've always liked the idea of adoption. If there are children who need families, why not make them mine? I never thought I could only love a child who came from my body."

"And if you have a child of your own someday?"

"I'd love all my children."

"And if you were in a rowboat that overturned, which child would you save?"

"The one that couldn't swim," they answered together.

"People ask the strangest questions, don't they?" Kyle said when they were done laughing. "I've been asked that so many times."

"How about this one." Angelle mimicked an old lady's voice. "If you get pregnant, dear, are you going to send the adopted child back?"

"No one has suggested that I might get pregnant," Kyle reminded her.

"Under the circumstances, you'd think they wouldn't suggest it of me either."

"Actually," Kyle said, with a slow survey of Angelle's slender body, "I imagine there are a number of men out there who are heartbroken that you won't consider it."

She blushed. She could feel the heat surging up to the roots of her blond hair, and she couldn't believe it was happening. After all the outrageous things he had said to her, she was blushing at a compliment. She tried to ignore it.

"That may well be, but unless my life changes drastically, pregnancy will be impossible." Good Lord, what had she just said? It sounded as though she was bemoaning her innocence instead of merely commenting on her unmarried state. A new wave of heat surged up to join the lingering traces of her first blush. She peeked at Kyle, who was swallowing convulsively.

"Angel, are you trying to tell me something?" he asked finally, suppressed laughter lingering on the edges of his question.

"I meant that I have no intention of getting married," she snapped. "I wasn't proclaiming my purity."

"I'll bet you are, though. Pure, I mean. As untouched as the white foam on those waves out there." He gestured toward the lake.

"Can you smell it? Is it written in indelible ink on my forehead?" she asked with anger in her voice. "How on earth would you know?"

"There's nothing to be ashamed of, Angel. Virginity is much admired in many parts of the world. And even if it's a trifle unusual at your age, well, more power to you."

She slid her chair back with one ferocious movement. "You are insufferable." As she leaped up from her chair, Kyle's fingers wrapped around her wrist.

"Simmer down, little lady. I'm not sure how we got on the subject, but accusing you of being a virgin is not exactly a class A insult. Would you like me to apologize? I'm sorry I suggested that you haven't slept with every man who comes down the pike." He tugged at her wrist, his fingers firmly twined around it. "Friends again?"

She sat down with a thud. "Am I the only one who's confused by this conversation?" she asked finally. "Don't answer that," she said as Kyle opened his mouth to speak. She removed her wrist from his grasp. "Let's hear why you're planning to adopt. Then we'll discuss your virginity . . . or lack of it." She leaned back, arms folded, and smiled.

"I love kids. I don't intend to ever get married . . . again, so I decided to try to adopt. I've been a Big Brother for years, and when my little foster brother moved away, it left a huge gap in my life. I want to be a father this time around."

Against her will, Angelle could picture Kyle with a little boy, tossing a football, putting together plastic models, flying kites. Instinctively she knew that he would be a terrific dad. "There are too few men out there who care about kids that much," she admitted with reluctant admiration. "Your son will be lucky."

Kyle smiled a little lopsided grin, and Angelle could almost see wheels turning in his head. "You'll make a good mother too," he said. "You're so all-fired vehement about everything. You'll be sure your daughter gets the best life has to offer."

Angelle basked in the strange compliment. "Tell me," she said when the silence had gone on too long and there was no Coke left to sip. "You mentioned that you were married before. Is that subject taboo?"

"No, but the marriage should have been."

"Bad experience?"

"One I'll never repeat." He folded his hands on the table and leaned toward Angelle. "Marriage is hell. You've got the right idea; it should be avoided at all costs."

"Tell me about it." The words slipped out before she had time to think about them. Why was she asking Kyle to share such a personal experience?

"It was years ago, while I was a Saint. Dale, my ex-wife, loved the limelight, and I thought I loved her." He laughed with no humor. "My knee was injured during my third year as a pro. With a lot of therapy and work, I could have been put back in good enough shape to stay on the team, but I decided that I had experienced enough pain. I chose to end my contract. Dale couldn't forgive me for that. She divorced me six months later."

"Oh, Kyle." Angelle covered his hands with hers. "What kind of woman was she?"

"Actually, she was a lot like you."

Angelle pulled her hands away. "Time for me to go."

"Or at least I thought so until tonight."

"And now?"

"Dale would never have cared about adopting a child. She never cared about anything except primping and changing her clothes and having her picture taken. She was little, like you, and very feminine. She was a redhead—though I hear she's a brunette now—and she was as sweet as all get-out, on the surface, that is. You're as pretty as she was, but I've discovered I was wrong about the sweetness. There's nothing sweet about you, Angel. You give as good as you get, and I like that."

It was another strange compliment.

"Kyle, am I imagining it, or are we beginning to understand each other, maybe even respect each other a little bit?" Unconsciously, she flashed her dimples at him.

"Well, I don't think the air is going to hum with suppressed animosity anymore. Maybe we've moved beyond the point where our hostility will affect the adoption process." Kyle held out a hand to help her out of her seat as he stood.

"Care to walk along the shore a ways? If I sit too long, my knee bothers me."

She should have said no; now that they were on speaking terms, she should have left it at that. But for some reason that she didn't understand, strolling with Kyle along the lakeshore was too pleasant to refuse.

Walking beside Kyle was very different from sitting with him, a table between them. The physical dissimilarities of their bodies were so prominently displayed when they were side by side that Angelle found herself feeling dwarfed. Actually, Kyle wasn't the tallest man Angelle knew, but he was the most solid, the most well muscled. He was a veritable granite wall.

"How do you keep in such good shape now that you're not out on the football field training every day?" she asked after they had walked in silence for a while.

"I do different things. I exercise, take long walks, swim. But my job keeps me fit. I like to get out and work with my crew whenever I get the chance. There's nothing like physical labor to keep you in shape."

Angelle wrinkled her nose. "You sound like my brother John. He owns a landscaping business, and if he's not outside all day, every day, he goes crazy. He used to drag me outside in all kinds of weather when we were kids and make me play with him."

"You have a brother?" Kyle sounded surprised. "Somehow I would have expected nothing except sisters."

"Three brothers, no sisters . . . and no mother. She died when I was barely a year old."

"That must have been rough."

"But look how well I turned out anyway."

She wished she hadn't said it quite that way when she felt him giving her a long perusal.

"Let's sit here for a few minutes, then I have to get going." Kyle took her arm and guided her to the cement seawall. They sat resting their feet on the concrete steps going down to the water. The lake was calm and the sky was star studded. There was nothing but water and air and winking celestial bodies. Surprised at her own reaction, Angelle felt at peace with the world.

"I'm glad you thought of this," she told Kyle. "I haven't come here since I was a teenager. Ending up here when somebody got the family car was a tradition."

"I was probably parked in the car next to yours."

"I was always with a bunch of girls. Giggling girls."

"Funny thing, I was always with a bunch of girls too," Kyle said with relish.

"I'll bet you were a wicked teenager. I'm surprised I never ran into you," Angelle said.

They began to trade names of schools they had attended, friends they had known, places they had hung out.

"Amazing," Kyle said when they had run out of details to share. "You knew everyone I knew, went everywhere I went, did everything I did..."

"With some notable exceptions I'm sure," she put in.

"I'm sure," he said with a grin, "but I don't think we ever met."

"I was younger and forgettable."

"I doubt it." Kyle turned to her and put his powerful hands on each side of her small face. "I would probably have fallen head over heels in love with you, Angel."

"Me and the rest of the females in New Orleans," she joked. But Kyle didn't laugh.

"No, except for Dale, I was always very careful about who I fell in love with."

"I just don't fall in love at all; it's easier that way," Angelle said, her breath coming in short spurts.

Kyle moved closer, his thumbs making a slow rotation under her chin. She knew that he could monitor her rapidly accelerating heartbeat, and she tried to pull away. It was useless.

"Never? You've never been in love? Why not?"

"I've never wanted to be."

"You've never wanted a man?"

"I've never wanted the things that come with a man."

"What things?" Kyle was steadily eating up the distance between them. She could feel his warm breath on her mouth and smell the clean citrus tang of his cologne.

"Dirty sweat socks, Monday night football, steak and potatoes..." She put her hands up to push him away and contacted the heated skin of his chest. When his mouth found hers, she was running her fingertips over the crisply curling auburn hair she had discovered, wondering why it felt so good, so natural to touch him.

His kiss felt good too. He didn't kiss like Dennis, her standby boyfriend. Dennis kissed with his mouth closed, and his kisses were sparing and well spaced. Kyle kissed with his mouth slightly open. His kisses were wet, and hot, and full-bodied. She knew that if she continued to cooperate, Kyle's kisses would be close together, melting one into the other until she screamed for mercy. If she did.

She planned to stop before that happened. That rational, well-thought-out part of her, the "adult," as Mrs. Simpson would say, was going to put a stop to this nonsense. But the "child" inside her, that emotional, irrational part of her, wouldn't let her stop. What Kyle was doing felt entirely too good.

Her fingers crept up his shoulders and around his neck, and she tangled them in the spilling curls that rested on his collar. His hair was soft and clung to her fingers, and as she tunneled her hands through it, his tongue parted her lips, teasing the soft skin inside them until she gasped and his tongue entered her mouth.

This kind of kissing was a whole new ball game, and Angelle knew it was time to put a stop to it. Still, she didn't. Kyle pulled her closer, and she could feel the buttons of his shirt straining through the soft buttercup silk of her dress. Her breasts flattened against him, and she could feel them swell until she thought she might burst with the pressure and the pleasure.

Kyle wrapped his arms around her back and pulled her even closer. His kiss deepened, and she was sure she was being swallowed alive, absorbed into his being. And strangely, it felt perfectly natural, as if they really were one body, two parts of a whole.

He broke the contact, finally, and with great reluctance. A series of smaller kisses punctuated the end of their closeness. We're done, they seemed to say, but I don't want to be.

Angelle pillowed her head on his chest, and he held her against him for a long time. With her ear so close to his heart, she could hear it speeding until it finally began to slow down and become more regular. She knew that her own matched it. She was too embarrassed to look at him. Along with her regular heartbeat, her regular good sense was reestablishing itself. What on earth was she doing?

It seemed like a perfectly good question to ask him. "What on earth are we doing?" she finally said when the question had become too big to answer internally.

"I think we're letting the moon get to us."

Angelle pulled away and wriggled to one side so that they weren't touching anymore. "There's no moon tonight."

Kyle was silent. "Angelle," he said finally, "I don't want a woman in my life. And certainly not one who's been keeping herself as pure as the driven snow. You're going to get hurt if you kiss me like that again."

She couldn't believe it. Back to square one. "What a rotten thing to say! Whose big hairy hands were on my face forcing me to endure that kiss?"

"Who ran her sharp little fingernails down my chest until my skin was so sensitized it resembled a mine field?"

"Who burrowed into my mouth like a groundhog in winter?"

"Who pressed her soft little body against mine like ... like..."

"A woman?"

"Exactly!"

"Me. And you loved every second of it, you big crazy Irishman." She stood on the steps for a second, shaking her finger at him. "Take your own advice, Kyle Sullivan. Even a fortress can get knocked down to size. Don't let youself get hurt." She stepped over the seawall and disappeared into the night.

Kyle watched her go, reluctantly admiring the way she twitched her hips. The little lady could almost make him forget that he didn't want a little lady in his life at all.

Chapter Four

At odd moments during the next week, Angelle remembered Kyle's kiss and her own reaction to it. She remembered the feel of his curls twined around her fingers and the warmth of his body as he held her against him. The kiss was confusing. Her reaction was even more so. She was twenty-six, innocent but not naive. There had been men in her life. Take Dennis, for example.

Perhaps that was the difference, she admitted ruefully. There had been a procession of Dennises but never a Kyle. Never anyone faintly resembling Kyle.

"My taste has always been impeccable. So why did that football-kicking Irishman catch me off guard?" She was mumbling to herself, her mind unalterably fixated on the events that had occurred a week before. It was Wednesday night, and she was climbing the stairs to the eighth floor of the ECS building. The elevator was being repaired.

To prove to Kyle that she was not the female stereotype that he believed her to be, she was wearing the most casual outfit that she could bear to buy. A mauve plaid blouse was tucked into wheat-colored cotton jeans. She was wearing cordovan top-siders to complete the picture. Never mind that she had bought them all that day; Kyle would never know.

Not that she was trying to impress Kyle Sullivan. Not at all. But it would be nice if he realized that he was wrong about her. She would like that. Making Kyle realize that he wasn't always right would be a pleasure.

A loud clatter sounded behind her, and a looming shadow crept up the wall to her side. Angelle didn't like deserted staircases any more than she liked parking garages. She was a little early for the home-study session, however, and she had seen no one else as she trudged up the stairs. Was that a moan? A ghostly shriek resounded through the stairwell. With a burst of speed, she took the steps two at a time heading for the sixth floor exit.

"I'm sorry, Angel. I couldn't resist." The disembodied voice floated up from the ramp below her.

Angelle stopped, taking a deep breath to calm her speeding heart. "Irish wit, Kyle? I can do without it."

"I caught sight of you a minute ago. You looked so serious, so lost in thought, so tired. Nothing like a little adrenaline to get you up the last two flights." He joined her on the step as he finished his sentence.

She saw immediately that wearing flat shoes was a mistake. Kyle towered over her, making her feel even more tiny, more delicate. She could dress like a lumberjack and his impression of her would not change one iota. They were different. Completely different. There was nothing to be done about it.

"Having you ascribe charitable motives to your bullying does not surprise me." Somehow she couldn't find the energy to say the words with much of a bite. That kiss, that glorious, outrageous kiss, had sapped her sarcasm.

"Come on, Angel. Where's your sense of humor? Here, I'll help you up the next two flights as penance." Kyle wrapped his strong arm around her waist and began to pull her along beside him. "Did you shrink, Angel? Did I grow?"

"Different shoes," she muttered. She should put a stop to this intimate contact, but her traitorous body was enjoying it too much.

"So how did the little lady spend her week besides buying new shoes?" Kyle pulled her closer as they started up the last flight.

She had no intention of mentioning that at least some part of the week had been spent thinking of him. "I was busy consulting for several weddings I'm coordinating."

"You wouldn't be helping with the Clayton Riley wedding, would you?" He dropped his arm and reached around to open the door for her.

"Yes. I am."

"It figures." Kyle followed her through the door and into the hallway. "Did you know that—"

"That you're the best man? Yes, I know."

"It's funny, Angel. All those years I never saw your pretty little face, and suddenly you know how to track me down everywhere I go."

Angelle tilted her nose and counted slowly to one hundred. She was inside the ECS conference room, sitting in a chair across the room from Kyle before she felt that it was safe to stop biting her tongue.

Angelle managed to avoid Kyle during the next two sessions. They were thrown together as partners once when they filled out a questionnaire about the kinds of problems they could accept in a child. The questionnaire was so involving, so thought provoking that there had been no time to trade quips or needle each other. They had acted like reasonable, intelligent adults, proving that it was possible if they both used extreme caution and forebearance.

Still, Angelle often found herself sneaking looks in Kyle's direction. Like to a magnet, her eyes were drawn to his healthy, unabashedly masculine body. Sometimes she would find that he was watching her too. Once she found him examining her soft curves, encased that night in a pink silk blouse and gray pants that did nothing to hide what her body had to offer. Kyle shot her an irritated glance that was a reflection of her own feelings. Why, it said, am I thinking about you? You are the last person in the world that I want to be attracted to.

She noticed when he cut his hair, and her fingers itched to stroke the shorter curls. She noticed that he never once smoked during any of the sessions, and she was glad to see that he wasn't hopelessly addicted to cigars. She noticed that he favored knit shirts to dress shirts, earth tones to brighter colors, loafers to shoes that laced. She noticed that his healthy tan brought out the brilliant turquoise of his eyes. Finally during the next-to-the-last session she noticed that she was noticing entirely too much.

Several of the couples had dropped out of the group, realizing that adoption wasn't for them. The group was smaller and more intimate now than it had been when it started, and Angelle was beginning to suffer withdrawal symptoms. She had gotten used to being there on Wednesday nights, on sharing her thoughts and feelings with these people, and she was going to miss them. And she had to admit it: she was going to miss Kyle most of all. He had brought a certain spice to her life that had been missing before.

As if he had been having similar thoughts, Kyle was staring at her when she turned to look at him. His expression could only be characterized as one of annoyed interest. She was sure that her expression was exactly the same.

When the session ended, Angelle stood, preparing to leave. She took her time smoothing her pleated beige skirt. When she looked up, Kyle was standing beside her. She raised her huge blue eyes to his face and smiled tentatively.

"I'm going to miss this group," she said. "How about you?"

"Yes." He continued to stand gazing down at her as if he wished she wasn't there, but his close proximity said something else entirely.

His apparent ambivalence would have been amusing if it hadn't been a mirror of what she was feeling herself. Finally she spoke. "Did you want something, Kyle?"

She could almost hear him grit his teeth. "I was wondering if you'd like to go out with me tomorrow night."

Why on earth was her heart leaping at the suggestion of a date with Kyle Sullivan? The normally sedate organ felt like a bullfrog with an alligator in hot pursuit. She was suddenly angry at her own response. This was Kyle. An evening with him would be spent trading insults, biting her tongue, fending off passionate advances. Her heart leaped again at the last thought.

And where would they go? To a football game? A wrestling match? A cock fight? She reached up to play with the bow of her violet blouse, rolling it in her fingers as she thought about his offer. With such a catalogue of possible disasters awaiting her on a date with him, why then did she still want to go?

"Your enthusiasm is overwhelming," he said dryly, watching the flickering expressions on her face.

"I'm sorry, Kyle, but I'm going to be busy tomorrow night catching up on paperwork at the shop. I've let myself get too far behind recently." There was a lot of paperwork, and she probably would spend the next evening doing it, especially since she had just told Kyle that she would.

Perhaps if he had pushed the matter, named another possible date, her defenses would have crumbled and she would have done what her heart was suggesting. She wasn't surprised, though, when he didn't. "All right," he said with a nod. In a moment he was gone.

Undoubtedly it was for the best. But like the bullfrog finally caught by the alligator, Angelle's heart died a little, and she looked out into the empty hallway feeling saddened and alone.

The shop was closed the next evening, and Angelle was just beginning to get her account books reorganized when the telephone rang. Ten minutes later she was on her way home to change clothes. Dennis had been given two tickets to the symphony by one of his accounting clients, and restlessly trying to fight off her lingering sadness at turning down Kyle's invitation, Angelle told Dennis that she would go with him.

At home she fed Miaou and searched her closet for something to wear. Finally she pulled out a sheer white cotton dress that was shot with hundreds of glistening silver threads. The dress had flowing, pleated sleeves and tiny pleats fell from the scooped neckline. Around her slender waist she fastened a thin silver belt and put on silver sandals to match. The dress emphasized her white-blond hair and pink-and-white complexion. With a trace of disgust, she decided that she looked like a child's Biblical illustration. "Angel in prayer."

When Dennis drove up Angelle was ready to go, and she watched him as he walked up the sidewalk. Dennis was very good-looking in a young-professional sort of way. He had smooth brown hair and even features. He was tall and slim, and he always wore a suit. She imagined that he even wore one to bed, although she had never had any desire to find out.

She opened the door and he leaned over to kiss her cheek. He always kissed it in precisely the same spot, with precisely the same amount of pressure, for precisely the same amount of time. Tonight that irritated her more than it should have. With a twinge of mischief, she turned her cheek just as his mouth descended, placing her lips beneath his. Afterward she realized that he had been oblivious to the change; Dennis had not known the difference.

"Would you care for some wine?" she asked politely.

He looked at his watch. Dennis always consulted his watch before he did anything. "I think we have time," he answered.

Angelle poured him a small glass and listened to his discussion of the merits of fine California Chablis compared to fine French Chablis. Angelle, who had trouble telling good vinegar from the finest wines available, just smiled. Dennis consulted his watch again, and Angelle found her shawl. A half hour later they were at the Orpheum, home of the New Orleans Symphony.

The Orpheum, a historic landmark, had been built at the beginning of the century as a vaudeville theater. Like many buildings of its ilk, it had been converted to a movie house and finally slated for demolition. But the proud old building with its classically inspired polychrome terra-cotta facade and its beaux arts style theater cried out for renovation. A committee stepped in to save it. Several large donations later, the Orpheum was well on its way to becoming another point of pride for the Crescent City.

Tonight the seats that Dennis had been given were in the back of the second balcony, and Angelle cautiously followed him up the steep steps, trying to forget that high places made her dizzy. Once she was seated she took out her opera glasses, a wise investment for any woman who dated Dennis. Dennis never went to the symphony or the opera or the theater unless he was given tickets. And invariably those tickets were in the last row. Angelle had resigned herself to his inability to spend money. He was an undemanding, acceptable escort. Dennis was a safe person to be with, and Angelle had always thought that safe was important.

They were a little early, and after chatting comfortably with Dennis for a few moments, Angelle began to examine the individual symphony members. After she had watched them for a while, she trained her glasses on the people sitting on the extreme sides of the theater. Their seats were some of the best in the house, perched higher than the ordinary seats in the orchestra section. Invariably they were held for the season by some of New Orleans' finest, and Angelle liked to see if any of her customers were there.

She recognized one woman wearing a dress that she had bought from Angelle the week before. Even more interesting was the face of the man behind her. Wreathed in careless brown curls that glowed with red glints under the soft theater lights was the profile of Kyle Sullivan.

Angelle dropped the opera glasses into her lap. Kyle at the symphony. She would never have believed it was possible. Fighting off the feeling that he could see her too, she raised the glasses for another look. He was dressed in a dark brown suit, and although she couldn't see much, what she could see was impressive. His arm was casually draped over the seat next to him where a brunette wearing something dark green and revealing was sitting.

It could have been Angelle sitting there beside him. It *should* have been her. She had suspected him of asking her to a wrestling match, a cock fight, and instead it had been an invitation to the symphony. Her prejudices had run away with her. The rational "adult" part of her that she prided herself on had led her astray. The "child" part of her wanted to cry.

The symphony was starting and Dennis was already beginning to fidget. Angelle knew that his musical interests ran to the piped-in music that played incessantly in his office waiting room. Dennis attended the symphony strictly because it was an opportunity to mingle with potential clients for his accounting firm. Dennis would never buy box seats, and he would never understand why anyone else did.

Angelle took one last look at Kyle. The expression on his face could only be classified as bliss. He was wrapped in the music that floated through the theater, letting it take him to the same places that it had often taken Angelle. In this one unsuspected way, they were kindred spirits. She settled down glumly, hoping that the music would exert its spell soon. At that moment all she could feel was misery.

When the house lights came back on for intermission, Dennis leaped up and grabbed Angelle's hand in an uncharacteristic display of affection. It turned out, however, that the hand holding was necessary to drag her swiftly through the crowd. "Dennis, where are we going?" she asked, trying to pull him to a stop.

"I want to get down to the lobby before the bulk of the crowd. I noticed a couple of people here that my firm has been trying to woo. I want to mingle."

"Well, I don't," she said, planting her feet firmly on the stairs. All she needed was to run into Kyle Sullivan in the lobby.

Dennis looked aghast. "You know how important this is to my career, Angelle. It's why I came tonight. It's why I brought you."

"I see. I'm good for your career too?"

"You certainly are when you behave. Now come on."

If she hadn't been wearing sandals, she would have kicked him. Never, never had she been even slightly serious about Dennis. But neither had she used him. She had thought they were friends enjoying a no-strings relationship. "I don't like being a pawn in your chess game, Dennis. I'm going back to my seat."

People were streaming past them, and Angelle tried gracefully to pull her hand from Dennis's grasp. But for once he was paying attention. "Look, I didn't mean it that way. Come on down to the lobby where we can talk." He turned and pulled her unwillingly down the steps behind him.

Once there she looked around the crowded room for Kyle, but he was nowhere to be seen. She relaxed slightly. Dennis came back with a glass of wine for her, and she waited for his apology.

"Look, Angelle. I thought that you and I had an understanding."

"Just what did we understand?"

"Well, I think we're right for each other. Basically we like the same things, know the same people, live the same lifestyle. We belong together. Sure, you're compatible with my image, but what's wrong with that? It won't hurt your business to be married to someone of my influence either."

"Married?" She choked on a sip of the wine.

"Certainly. As soon as we can afford a place in the Garden District near your brother Charles's house, I want us to marry. It's a sensible decision."

"I don't want to marry you, Dennis."

Dennis didn't even blink. "After you think about it, you'll see what a good idea it is."

"Dennis, the only time you ever mentioned marriage was when I told you I was going to adopt a child. Then you said you would never ask me if I went through with it. I'm going to adopt, and soon. What does that do to your carefully thought-out plans?"

His eyebrows came together in a frown. "Why would you want to adopt now? In four or five years we can start a family, a real family."

"Adoption is real." She finished her wine and smiled. "I'm the wrong woman for you, Dennis. But there are

plenty of women out there who are just as socially acceptable as I am. One of them will be thrilled with your offer."

To his credit, Dennis actually looked disappointed. "I
see," he said finally.

"Come on, you heart's not broken, Dennis," she said,
trying to cheer him up. "You're not in love with me. I'll
even introduce you to some suitable wifely prospects."

He brightened noticeably.

Angelle patted him on the cheek. "Now, I'm going back
upstairs. You mingle enough for both of us, all right?"

She started through the lobby toward the stairs when a
voice stopped her. "Don't run off, Angelle. I haven't had a
chance to talk to you tonight." The voice was deep and res-
onant, and unmistakably Kyle's.

It was with a sincere feeling of dread that she turned
around to face him. "Hello, Kyle."

He nodded. "I'm surprised to find you here."

"I'm surprised to be here. It was a last-minute decision."

"It must have been." Kyle gestured to a pretty brunette
who came up to stand beside him. "Angelle Reed, this is
Kate Peters."

Kate was lovely in a robust, healthy way. She had short
dark hair that cried out for a sweatband and a sun-kissed
complexion. Her dress was low-cut and slinky, revealing
long tanned legs that belonged under a tennis dress. She was
earthy and natural, everything that Kyle said he wanted in
a woman. No one would mistake Kate for a Bible illustration.

"Hello, Angelle." Kate was giving her a thorough once-
over, and Angelle waited until she was done before she responded.

"Hello, Kate. Are you enjoying the music?"

Kate shrugged. "I'm not much for classical music, but
Kyle loves it. I guess I'll learn." As if to emphasize her

claim, Kate took Kyle's arm and leaned against him. They were almost the same height.

"I'm looking forward to the Mozart Piano Concerto after intermission," Angelle continued. "I was just on my way back to my seat."

"Angelle, introduce me to your friends." Dennis came up beside her, looking as if the shock of her refusal to marry him had already worn off. He linked his arm in hers.

Angelle made the introductions reluctantly. Kyle was watching the proprietary way that Dennis treated her, and Angelle found herself wishing she could explain her relationship with Dennis to him. Dennis, for his part, was fawning over Kyle as if he was a celebrity.

"Are you Kyle Sullivan of Sullivan Construction?"

Kyle nodded, his eyes on Angelle.

"I'm with Posthill, Dunn and Ford. You've been considering employing our firm, I understand."

Angelle had to admit as Kyle and Dennis chatted that Dennis was a natural. He had a real knack for making the right kind of impression on a potential client. He was polite, respectful, interested. He was everything she had always thought she wanted in a man. She yawned, covering her mouth with a small hand.

"Are we keeping you up, Angelle?" Kyle asked.

"This conversation couldn't possibly keep anyone up," she said without thinking. Dennis squeezed her arm in warning.

Kyle smiled at her for the first time, and Kate moved closer to him as if to reassert her claim. "And what do you do, Angelle?" she asked.

"I run LaBois Bridal. How about you?"

"I teach physical education."

"Kate is a very physical person," Kyle said with a pat on the brunette's arm.

Angelle had no trouble believing it was true.

"Angelle hates exercise, don't you, honey?" Dennis asked her.

Dennis had never called her "honey" in their entire relationship. Evidently he had decided that since she knew Kyle, he would benefit professionally if he appeared to be intimate with Angelle. She shrugged, trying to pull her arm out of his grasp.

Dennis laughed and held on tightly. "The most strenuous thing I've ever seen her do is walk down the sidewalk to her car."

"That's a pity," Kyle said, watching her trying to squirm away from Dennis's grip. "Angelle just seems to be made for certain kinds of physical exercise."

His meaning was unmistakable to Angelle as she watched his eyes roam over her body. Obviously Kate also understood his reference. "Now, Kyle," the brunette scolded, "don't give Angelle any ideas. If she's not used to it, any kind of exercise would be a bad idea. Without some serious preparation," Kate added with a sly smile, "too much physical exertion could be fatal. And Angelle doesn't look prepared."

Dennis missed the innuendos completely. "I don't think you need to worry. Angelle isn't inclined that way anyhow."

Kyle choked, and Kate giggled. Angelle just lifted her nose in the air and succeeded in jerking her arm out of Dennis's grasp. "I'm charmed to meet one of Kyle's friends, Kate," she said with a nod to the brunette. "It's delightful to find that he has somebody his own size to play all his little games with." With a smile and another nod, she made her escape.

Angelle climbed the stairs and sat alone in the back row of the second balcony until Dennis joined her. Even when the Mozart Concerto began, filling the theater with some of her favorite music, Angelle still wished fervently that she had spent the evening balancing books.

Miaou was comfortably nestled on Angelle's white satin lap listening to Angelle hum Mozart as she brushed her silvery hair. The trip home from the symphony had been silent, with Dennis obviously irritated at her. Angelle was certain that his anger was more because she had not been friendly to Kyle and Kate than because she had told him she wouldn't marry him. There had been no good-night kiss.

Angelle had come inside, stripped off her dress and taken a long bath, finally putting on her favorite nightgown. The gown, made from white on white embroidered satin with a high Chinese collar and long drifting chiffon sleeves, had originally been intended for a bridal trousseau, but brides today wanted something more revealing, and Angelle had finally brought it home from the store for herself. Another angel's costume, she thought as she brushed her hair. Any minute I'm going to open my mouth and hosannas are going to pour forth.

It was late, but she wasn't tired. The interactions with Dennis and with Kyle had her mind whirling. Dennis she could dismiss fairly rapidly. He might think that marriage was convenient and practical for them, but he would recover quickly from her refusal. Her interaction with Kyle was another matter. She was very sorry that Kyle had seen her at the symphony. Never one for playing games with men, she wished that she had been straightforward with him when he had asked her out. Now she looked like a conniving femme fatale who had just been waiting for a better offer.

Her doorbell interrupted her self-flagellation. "Who is it?" she called. Late night visitors were rare, and she was struck with visions of bell-ringing burglars or Western Union messengers with ominous telegrams.

"Kyle."

She got up and peeked through the window. It was Kyle. He was still dressed in the brown suit, and he still looked terrific. "I'm coming." She unlocked the door and let him in.

"I saw your light. I hope I didn't wake you," he said.

"No, come sit down." She gestured him to the flowered chintz sofa. "How did you know where I lived?"

He was looking around the little living room, shaking his head. "I didn't know there were this many flower prints available in the whole world."

She had gone overboard on flowers. She admitted it. Sometimes the room was even too overwhelmingly feminine for her. But this was the first place she had ever been able to decorate to her taste, and she had put everything in it that she had ever wanted. It was a pink-and-white, ruffle-and-lace, flower-filled sanctuary.

"I like flowers. How did you know where to find me?"

"I drove down Calhoun until I saw your car parked out front. The scratched bumper was unmistakable, and if I had any doubts, the pink paint and the lavender gingerbread trim on this house were enough to put them to rest."

"Why are you here? Did you think of more obscene jokes to make at my expense?" She sat down on the edge of the sofa, laying her hairbrush on the table beside her.

He had the grace to look sheepish. "I guess I owe you an apology."

"I guess you do." She held up her hand before he could say anything. "I guess I owe you one too. Maybe we can just cancel each other out."

Kyle shrugged, leaning back against the soft cushions. "I don't really care about an apology, but I'd like an explanation."

Angelle was being given a chance to be frank with him, but suddenly she didn't know what to say. She did know that another lie wouldn't do, however. She tucked her feet up under the satin gown and stared at him for a long minute.

Kyle began to look irritated, more irritated in fact than the situation called for. Finally, as she was getting ready to try to explain herself, he broke the silence.

"Angel, do you have any idea how provocative you look right now?"

She blinked, trying to figure out what he meant. "How could anyone think this is provocative?" She pulled the heavy satin away from her body. "I'm as well covered up as if I was wearing granny's flannel bathrobe."

Kyle slid closer to her, gently trailing his finger along the row of satin buttons that ran from the collar to the hem of the gown. Angelle's stomach fluttered in response.

"This gown was made for a wedding night," he said softly.

Her voice was a squealing protest. "It's as opaque and impenetrable as a fall-out shelter!"

"It's exactly the kind of gown a man wants to see his bride in the first time he makes love to her." Kyle's finger slid back up the long row of buttons to the top and settled on the first button again. "Shall I tell you why?"

Mutely she shook her head, but Kyle paid no attention.

"When a man and a woman are finally alone, after a hectic, emotional, wedding day, and she comes out in something sheer and cut to here—" his other hand came to rest right below her breasts "—her new husband would be so wrought up, he'd pounce on her. He'd scare her to death too." The tip of Kyle's finger caught the loop behind the top button and began to tug gently.

"No man wants to start like that, Angel. No man wants a frightened bride. If she comes out in something like this, though, something that tells him to take it slow, to take it easy, then he's forced to take his time. He's forced to make it good for both of them." Slowly Kyle lifted his finger and the first button was freed.

"What are you doing?" she asked in a strangled voice. "Don't do this."

His hand paused on the second button. "I'm looking for answers, Angel." Deftly the second button and then the third were undone. At the same time, his other hand began to trace tiny circles right through the satin, burning the skin beneath. Kyle was watching the emotions flickering across her face, and she knew that her response was there for him to see.

The fourth button and the fifth followed the others. Carefully Kyle folded back the slippery material, baring the valley between her breasts. "You like this, don't you, Angel?" He bent his head and began to place tiny kisses on her neck, following the path of the buttons. She placed her hands on his shoulders to push him away, but she couldn't bear to exert any pressure. His fingers were undoing two more buttons, sliding the fabric away as he did.

"Stop, Kyle," she gasped. "No more."

"That's exactly what a new bride would say," he whispered, his mouth against her white skin. "And her husband would be content with this much, at least for a little while." Slowly his hand reached inside her gown and began to stroke the softness he had uncovered.

Angelle shivered, her body reacting to his gentle movements. She leaned her head back on the sofa and let him touch her, let him explore the contours of her breasts, let him feel her growing response. She expected him to kiss her, but he didn't, only placing soft nips along her neck and the side of her face. When she turned her mouth to his, he still didn't, seemingly content with just watching her.

"Do you like this, Angel? Do I make you feel good?"

She nodded, eyes half shut, reveling in his caresses.

"Say it."

"Yes," she moaned as he began to gently tug at her aroused nipple. "Yes, I like it."

"Good." His mouth tantalized hers, finally brushing her lips with his. He laughed softly as she tangled her fingers in his hair, holding him still to deepen the kiss. His fingers continued to apply subtle torture as his tongue swept her lips, signaling her to open her mouth. When she did, he played with her, teasing her with his tongue and his lips until she thought she would lose her mind with need for him.

It had never been like this before. It was not the first time a man had kissed her, not the first time a man had touched her. But it was the first time she had wanted to beg for more, and that realization shot fear-powered adrenaline through her body. But even with her system telling her it was time to quit, she couldn't make herself say a word.

Kyle moved back a fraction of an inch to look at her. "You're so beautiful in passion, Angel. Your skin heats up and you're rose-flushed and touchable. Not an unapproachable angel at all."

She shook her head slowly. "Kyle, we shouldn't . . ."

"Yes, we should. Can't you feel how right this is? I don't want it, you don't want it. But it's happening. Let it happen, Angel." When his mouth covered hers again she moaned, but whether in protest or surrender, she wasn't sure.

How could a kiss and a touch, two external events, have such a profound effect on what happened inside her? Kyle touched her and suddenly in her very depths were pulsating rhythms driving her to seek even greater pleasures. Kyle kissed her and she resonated in every cell, every particle. Like a complicated circuit board with an overload of electricity, her ability to reason shut down completely, leaving her to experience, to feel, with no guidance whatsoever.

Kyle too seemed to be heading for that dangerous place where instinct alone controls. And in the end, it was Kyle who refused to let it happen. He pulled away, taking his warmth and his tantalizing touch with him. Angelle felt bereft and grateful simultaneously. For a moment she just sat looking at him, and then, realizing how exposed she was, she pulled the edges of her gown back together and began to button it with trembling fingers.

"I don't understand you; I don't understand this," she said in a voice that sounded close to a wail.

"Is that why you told me you wouldn't go out with me?" Kyle asked quietly.

She nodded. "Kyle, there's something strange going on here. I don't want to feel this way about you."

"What way?"

"I think you know."

"Tell me," he insisted.

"I feel like I'm being run over by a truck and loving every minute of it." She finished fastening the gown and edged away from him. "You are not the kind of man I want in my life."

"You don't want a man in your life at all."

"That's not true," she protested.

"You want someone like Dennis?"

"Good Lord, no."

Kyle looked surprised. "You and Dennis aren't an item?"

"No. We aren't. I don't want Dennis in my life either."

"Why do you hate men?"

"Did I just act like I hate men?" she snapped. "I just don't think that you and I are compatible, Kyle. We have nothing in common. It's foolish to let a little thing like physical attraction pull us together when we aren't the same kind of people at all. We come from different worlds."

"The Irishman and the Creole? Angel and the Saint?" His eyes hardened, and he stiffened visibly. "Perhaps you're right," he said finally. "At least I hope I have nothing in common with a snobby, lying little lady who values her rarefied existence more than she values reality.''

She was hurt by his words, but she refused to let him see it. "I'm not a snob, and I think I'm a realist. At least I have the good sense to put a stop to something that would only hurt us both.''

"Angel, you'd put a stop to everything in the world that can't be tied up with a pretty pink ribbon if you were able to. You have no idea what reality is." He stood and gave her a mocking salute. "I'm glad we both know where we stand now. I won't bother you again.''

With her eyes tightly shut, Angelle heard the door slam and the roar of his cycle. When she could no longer hear his engine in the distance she continued to remain frozen in the same position. One lonely teardrop found its way down her nose, sliding off to mar the perfect white satin of her nightgown.

Chapter Five

Avoiding Kyle at the last home-study session was a simple matter. There was such an excess of goodwill and excitement among members of the little group that no one noticed Kyle and Angelle never got within ten feet of each other. With a great sense of purpose, Angelle wore a plain gray suit and a polite smile. When it was necessary to look in Kyle's direction, she found that he was ignoring her with a vehemence matched only by her own.

What should have been a warm ending to weeks of work and self-discovery left Angelle feeling strangely empty. Group members exchanged phone numbers and information that they had received from various out-of-state adoption agencies. Angelle promised several couples that she would call them when she received her referral, and she teasingly volunteered a night's baby-sitting for the first family who received their child. Still, it was with sadness that she made her way outside to her car when the group was over.

The tie that had connected Kyle Sullivan and Angelle Reed was broken. There would be no more nights spent trying to ignore each other, no more nights spent revealing personal feelings. They were free of each other. And freedom felt . . . lonely.

"You are definitely moping," Madame LaBois told Angelle a week later. "If I didn't know better I'd think you were sixteen again."

"I've just been working hard," Angelle defended herself.

Madame LaBois sniffed, her perfectly coiffured head bent over a large glass display case. "Moping!" she said, pulling her head up for an instant. "For all the world to see."

It was true. "It's disgusting, isn't it," Angelle conceded. "At sixteen I had an excuse. At twenty-six, I can't even blame my hormones."

"I wouldn't say that."

Angelle turned, pretending to minutely examine the flowers on a bridesmaid's straw hat, but she was too late—the rosy blush was there for her grandmother to read, and Madame LaBois pressed her advantage. "Why fight it, baby? If there's a man you're interested in, go after him."

"You've heard the expression 'playing with fire'? Well, with this man, it would be more like playing in an atomic mushroom cloud. I'd never come out of it alive."

"Changed maybe, but certainly alive. Kyle Sullivan isn't fatal."

"How did you know who I was talking about?"

Madame LaBois stood behind Angelle and slowly turned her around. "His name keeps coming up in your conversation." She took the wide-brimmed, flower-bedecked hat out of her granddaughter's hands and set it on Angelle's white-blond hair. "Always a bridal consultant, never a bride, Angelle. Not until you figure out what you want and go after it."

"It's too late, Maw Maw. I'm probably not even going to see him again."

"The Riley wedding."

Angelle nodded slowly. "Yes, but we'll both be so busy..."

"Find the time."

"I'm not sure I want to. I can't help believing that he's exactly the wrong person for me."

"And I can't help believing that makes him the perfect choice."

Angelle removed the hat and plopped it on her grandmother's head. "I should introduce you to Kyle. It would be love at first sight for both of you."

"I daresay there are a lot of women out there who would appreciate Kyle Sullivan."

That thought plagued Angelle for the rest of the afternoon.

Luckily, in the next week there were very few moments available to think about Kyle. Angelle's tenants had decided not to renew their lease, and she found herself cleaning and painting the other side of her house to ready it for potential renters.

She was down on her hands and knees scraping and waxing the old cypress floors when the telephone call that she had not expected to get for months came. Mrs. Simpson wanted to see her about a possible placement.

"I'm going to be a mother," she told Miaou with a whoop. "Somewhere in the world right now is a little girl who's going to be mine." She danced around the house, weaving in and out of the two apartments by the connecting door that was usually bolted on both sides. "Mine. All mine."

The sands of time seemed to stop their dribbling for the rest of the week. More than once, Angelle picked up the ornate quartz anniversary clock from the counter at LaBois Bridal and shook it the way a baby shakes a plastic rattle. The third time Madame LaBois saw her pick it up, she removed the glass and brass dome from Angelle's reach, replacing it with a dime store alarm clock. "For the duration," she said with a shake of her head.

Angelle, who was always patient and tactful with customers, could hardly wait to push them out the door when Friday came. Her appointment with Mrs. Simpson was for four o'clock, and Madame LaBois and a young woman who helped behind the counter finally asked Angelle to leave, claiming that she was scaring patrons away.

At three-thirty, Angelle found herself walking into the reception room at Ecumenical Children's Services wondering how she was going to survive the next half hour. She had dressed very carefully, having searched her wardrobe for the most maternal outfit that she owned. Since that concept was very ambiguous, she had finally settled on a skirt and blouse of a deep rose silk jersey. She wasn't sure that she really looked like somebody's mother, but she did feel feminine and that was a start.

Wanting to appear calm, she picked up a magazine and sat down on the sofa to read it. Only after she had been staring at it for ten minutes did she realize that she was reading *Sports Illustrated*. The article she had chosen featured profiles of retired football players.

Reminders of Kyle were everywhere. She had managed, for the most part, to push him out of her mind in the past weeks, but a day hadn't passed that she hadn't thought of him. When a motorcycle roared by, when she shopped for groceries or visited the park, when she heard Mozart, Kyle was there for her. She had not allowed herself to dwell on her feelings, but she was aware that eventually she'd have to look deeper.

"Angelle?"

She had been lost in thought, so lost that she hadn't heard the slam of an office door and footsteps that had come to rest in front of her chair. Looking up from the magazine, she caught the gleam of a heavy brass belt buckle fastening sleek gold corduroy pants. She counted the buttons on the cream-colored shirt. The top three were unbuttoned. The man's neck was strong and proud; the face was Kyle's. She had almost forgotten how attractive he was, and a half smile lit her face as she stared at him through gold-tipped lashes.

"Hi. I guess I was deep in thought."

Kyle's eyes flickered to the magazine article, and Angelle turned almost as pink as her outfit. It wouldn't take much detective work for him to figure out what thoughts she had been deep in. She slammed the magazine shut. "I'm surprised to see you," she said as nonchalantly as she could manage.

"I just finished an appointment with Mrs. Simpson."

Everything else was forgotten. Angelle jumped up, her turned-up nose an inch from his chest. "Tell me!"

If Kyle was surprised by her enthusiasm, he didn't let on. His smile was so broad that he was almost unable to speak. "I'm the father," he said proudly, "of a five-year-old Korean boy."

Angelle's arms shot around him in a bear hug that almost knocked him over. "Kyle! Kyle! Congratulations." She was jumping up and down, still hugging him tightly, until she realized that the effect of her small breasts pounding his chest could only be termed "erotic." She stepped back an inch or two to look at his face. "Tell me all about it!"

Kyle pulled her down to the sofa, his arm curled behind her. All the barriers that had been between them in the long weeks they had known each other dissolved. They were man and woman, sharing their love of children, their reverence for life. "And so," Kyle finished, "Mrs. Simpson saw him at the orphanage and decided to find a home for him. I walked in a week after she got back from Korea and told her that I was looking for a little boy, four years old or up, and I didn't care where he came from or what his background was. She said it was like the Irish Sweepstakes, and I walked in with the lucky number."

"So everything fit perfectly for you," Angelle crowed. "It's fate. You were meant to be his father."

"It feels that way. There wasn't anyone else on her list who was looking for a child that fit his description. Otherwise I could have waited a long time."

Angelle grasped Kyle's hand and gave it a warm squeeze. "Mrs. Simpson knew a good bet when she saw you, Kyle. Single or not, she knew you'd be a wonderful parent. I'm so happy for you." Without thinking, she lifted his hand to her cheek, stroking it against her soft skin. And that one simple, sensual act changed everything.

When Angelle realized what she was doing, and with whom, she dropped his hand immediately. But Kyle's fingers lingered to trace the tilt of her nose, the curve of her cheekbone. "Thank you, Angel, for being here to share this with me. You're probably the only person I know who really understands."

Angelle's heart had lodged permanently in her throat, threatening to cut off her air supply. "I'm glad I could be here," she finally croaked.

Kyle straightened and sat back, removing his hand with noticeable reluctance. "And why are you here?"

"Mrs. Simpson wants to talk to me about a placement too."

"We're both going to be parents, it seems," he said with another grin. "The little lady is going to be a little mother."

"And the big football player is going to start his very own team."

He told her of his plans to end his present lease and buy a house, and she told him she'd keep her eyes open since he wanted to stay in the same neighborhood. The words were friendly, but Angelle could almost feel the powerful electricity crackling in the air between them. She wanted nothing more than to admit to Kyle that she noticed it, that she was susceptible to it. She also knew that statement would send her life careering down a path she was afraid to consider.

They were staring at each other. Angelle knew that her private struggle was there for Kyle to read if he chose to. In his eyes she saw a similar battle. She cleared her throat. "Well," she started.

She wasn't sure what she was going to say, but before she had a chance to trip over her own tongue, Mrs. Simpson stuck her head out of her office door. "Angelle? I'm ready when you are."

"I have to go," she murmured, collecting her purse.

"Good luck," Kyle said, standing with her.

"Thanks." As she got to the office door, she turned, wondering if Kyle would wait to find out about her new daughter, but he was gone. The disappointment she felt was as strong as the electricity that had surged between them.

Inside Mrs. Simpson's office, Angelle quickly forgot about anything except the reason for being there. She took a seat and listened as the adoption worker told her about her new daughter. The little girl was three, a Korean orphan, with a minor medical problem that would require physical therapy and lots of good food.

"I thought of this child the first time I met with you, Angelle. She'll need tons of special attention and care, and I knew right away that she'd get them from you. It didn't hurt that your brother Michael is a pediatrician either."

"The Irish Sweepstakes again." Angelle said with ear-to-ear dimples. "I was in the right place at the right time."

"Adoption is like that," Mrs. Simpson admitted. "We can't just keep lists and match children and parents by numbers. It's not always first come, first served. Obviously we're not concerned about hair color and skin tones like adoption agencies were decades ago, because there just aren't that many children available now. No, now we're concerned about the best way to meet everyone's needs. Sometimes if a child and a grown-up are right for each other, it just jumps out at us. Unscientific maybe, but that's how it works.

"I feel so blessed."

"This adoption is a big step forward for all of us. We hope to begin using more single parents and placing more older children. There's a startling need for parents for teenagers." Mrs. Simpson smiled and handed Angelle a photograph. "Here's your daughter, Angelle. Meet Jin Ah."

The little girl had the saddest face Angelle had ever seen. Her dark eyes were enormous, taking up half her pixie face. Her hair was cut short, emphasizing hollow cheeks, and her mouth was turned down as if she wanted to cry. Angelle fell in love immediately. "I feel like I know her already," Angelle said, reverently tracing the tiny features on the photograph.

"I wouldn't have chosen a working mother for her, but since you're planning to keep her with you at the shop until she's school age, I'm sure it will work out."

"I'm going to furnish one of our storerooms as a play area. I don't plan to miss another minute of her life that I don't have to."

Mrs. Simpson gave Angelle a list of the necessary steps to initiate the adoption. "There's more paperwork than you can imagine, and this won't happen quickly. It will be months before she arrives."

"I'll try to be patient, and I'll start filling out forms today."

Angelle stood, clutching the photograph. "I can't thank you enough."

"You have no idea how much pleasure this gives me." Mrs. Simpson stood up and shook Angelle's hand. "I think I have the best job in the world."

Angelle turned in the doorway. "You know, a few minutes ago I saw Kyle in the waiting room. Does his child come from the same orphanage as mine?"

Mrs. Simpson nodded. "Yes, I met them both there."

Another common bond between two people who seemed to have nothing in common at all. Music, two orphaned Korean children and electricity that only got more pronounced at each meeting. Angelle waved goodbye, muttering to herself about the twists of fate.

She was still muttering about fate when the next Friday rolled around and she prepared to attend the Riley wedding rehearsal. Susan Berry, soon to be Riley, had spent long hours with Angelle, consulting on every aspect of the ceremony. Angelle had been consultant, friend and psychologist with hardly a moment to herself.

Susan, a pretty, dark-haired wraith, had gone through New Orleans' own Newcomb College with Angelle, and the two women had remained in touch. Susan's wedding was part business, part pleasure. Angelle had given it her all.

With the realization that Kyle would be present, Angelle took extra care dressing, wearing a blue crepe dress that exactly matched her eyes, and heels high enough to make her feel at less of a disadvantage. Then, after taking long minutes doing makeup and sweeping her hair into a sophisticated knot on top of her head, she prepared to ignore him.

He was, of course, difficult to ignore. She arrived at the City Park rose garden, acres of roses in the midst of one of the largest city parks in the United States, and promptly sought out the minister who would be performing the ceremony. Together they discussed arrangements for seating, for the procession and recession and for music. She was still talking to the congenial young clergyman when she felt a pair of eyes burning a hole through her crepe-clad back. Without turning around, she knew that Kyle had arrived.

When the minister excused himself to greet the bride and groom, Angelle took a breath and faced Kyle. He was standing next to a lovely brunette who could have been Kate Peters's sister, his arm wrapped around her waist. Angelle recognized the woman; she was Susan's maid of honor, and Angelle had done the fitting for her dress.

"Hi, Angelle," the brunette said. "Have you met Kyle Sullivan yet?"

Angelle pinned a friendly smile on a face that didn't really want to budge. "Yes, thank you, Lisa. Hello, Kyle."

Kyle inclined his head. "How are you, Angelle?"

Ready to dig a hole and pull it in over me, she thought. Kyle and Lisa went together like steamboats and the Mississippi, like coffee and chicory, like red beans and rice. She ran out of other New Orleans analogies. No matter. The point had been firmly made. Lisa looked as if she belonged in the crook of Kyle's arm, and Angelle felt a sense of loss that almost knocked her over. "I'm fine," she said, turning to look for Susan. "Nice to see you both." And it would have been true . . . if she hadn't seen them together.

It's all right, she told herself as she helped herd everyone to the spot where the wedding was to take place. She had come that night, unsure what she should do about Kyle Sullivan. With all her heart she wanted to do nothing, to ignore the magnetism he held for her, to go on with her safe existence. But magnetism was difficult to ignore. It pulled, it tugged, it placed you in funny positions you didn't necessarily want to be in. If Kyle was exerting all that energy in another direction, it would be easier to forget him.

The rehearsal went fine. The minister, Dr. Reynolds, had confided to Angelle that this was his first outdoor wedding. Because Angelle had done dozens, she participated more than usual, making suggestions and guiding the wedding party to try different formations until Susan and Clayton were satisfied. She explained to the ushers what would be expected of them, taught the bridesmaids how to pace their procession, showed Lisa exactly when to begin her march down the aisle and snuck a piece of hard candy to the fidgeting flower girl.

Guiding Kyle was more difficult. Obviously pretending to be obtuse, he misunderstood her directions time and time again until she had to take him by the arm and lead him through his paces. The one point that seemed perfectly clear to him was that he got to escort Lisa back down the aisle at the ceremony's end. He did so with ungentlemanly enthusiasm.

"One more run-through," Dr. Reynolds said with a clap of his hands. "This time we'll practice a bit of the ceremony."

"That's bad luck!" Susan was adamant. She had watched the rehearsal from the sidelines, having refused so far to even walk down the aisle on her father's arm.

"I just want to make sure that everyone knows when they're supposed to do things," Dr. Reynolds explained. "This is a fairly complicated ceremony."

"It's bad luck." Susan would not be thwarted. "Can't you use a stand-in?"

And so it was that Angelle Reed walked down the make-believe aisle clutching a make-believe father's arm to stand beside a make-believe groom and Kyle Sullivan. The bridal couple had decided to follow a complicated path through the rose garden out to the shade of live oak trees draped with Spanish moss where the ceremony was to be held. To Angelle's surprise, Kyle didn't take his eyes off her once, not even with the willowy Lisa gliding right in front of her. The moment was golden.

The ceremony, a mixture of the traditional and the contemporary, was designed to touch the emotions of everyone observing. When Angelle was finished pretending that she was marrying Clayton Riley, she turned to see Kyle's expression and noted that he too had been moved. His dark turquoise eyes were focused on her as if he was trying to memorize each of her delicate features. He smiled, an enigmatic smile that softened his rugged face and made him strangely vulnerable. The look he gave her was no less intimate than the look a proud groom would give his beloved bride. Without understanding exactly why, it seemed to Angelle that something momentous had just occurred, and not for Clayton and Susan.

When it was time for everyone to drive to a French Quarter Hotel for the rehearsal dinner, it was Lisa's arm that Kyle took, and Lisa who climbed into the front seat of the Red Volvo station wagon that Kyle was driving. The lonely ten-minute drive was just long enough for Angelle to make an earthshaking decision. She was going to let Kyle know, somehow, that she missed him and that she no longer felt that they were *completely* incompatible.

That moment at the makeshift altar had been the final signal to the part of her that had been fighting Kyle all along. She could no longer ignore what she felt. Kyle Sullivan was not the man for her. She was still convinced of that. But she could no longer pretend that she wasn't attracted to him. He was on her mind entirely too much.

The only way that she knew to cure that phenomenon was to spend more time with him. Intimacy was a sure-fire cure for attraction. Once she stopped trying to avoid him, she was sure that avoiding him would become simple. They would both go their separate ways, glad that they had the sense to see they weren't right for each other.

She thought about telling Kyle her motivation for seeking him out. "Let's get each other out of our systems. Then we can resume our normal existence," she could say. Still, that approach didn't seem too flattering, and Kyle obviously had an ego that needed stroking. She decided not to explain herself at all. That made approaching him more difficult, but she was sure she could think of a way.

The first part of her plan was to try to sit near Kyle at the dinner. When she arrived, however, she discovered that the seating arrangement had been taken care of by hotel staff. She was at a table far from Kyle with Dr. Reynolds and his wife and two of Clayton's uncles from out of town.

The dinner was delicious, fine Creole cuisine with some of Angelle's favorite dishes. The hotel atmosphere was charming, with red plush carpeting, mahogany antiques and impeccable service. Her tablemates were friendly, and the occasion a joyous one for everyone except Angelle, who felt strangely as if she were at a funeral.

The seating arrangement was understandable. Angelle had been to enough rehearsal dinners to realize that. What wasn't understandable was the way that Kyle and Lisa kept their heads together all night, talking, laughing, exchanging what Angelle could only term "meaningful looks." Kyle and Lisa were enjoying themselves immensely. By dessert a depressed Angelle wondered if Lisa would be calling her soon to plan Lisa's own wedding to Kyle.

The evening culminated in numerous champagne toasts to the bride and groom, including one that Kyle made.

"To love," he said looking straight at Lisa, who was sitting beside him. "And to the circumstances that draw people together."

Angelle was not sure if it was the toast or just one glass of champagne too many that gave her the headache that she drove home with that night. What she was sure of was that she had missed her chance with Kyle Sullivan.

Had she been anyone else, Angelle could have avoided attending the wedding and reception the next day. She had awakened with a continuation of her headache and a firm desire to stay in bed indefinitely, but she had a full day's work to do before she went to Susan's house to help the bride and her attendants prepare for the ceremony.

For the first time in her life, Angelle was tired of her job. Where once she would liked to have dressed every New Orleans bride in LaBois finery, today she was irritated that anyone would even walk through the shop door. With her grandmother muttering about hormones again and the other shop personnel trying to protect customers from Angelle's attentions, she finally left, her car stuffed with last-minute paraphernalia for the wedding.

The driveway in front of Susan's one-story brick home in the Lakeview section of New Orleans was completely full, and Angelle had to park halfway down the street. Grumbling, she carried stacks of boxes up the front sidewalk, ringing the doorbell with her elbow.

Inside, the commotion was unbelievable. The tiny house was packed with people. Every out-of-town relative, every in-town friend had dropped by to help. Try as she might to hang on to her bad mood, Angelle was swept away by the excitement. She visited with friends from college that she hadn't seen in years, sampled reception hors d'oeuvres, drank prewedding champagne and gave good sound advice. It was only when she was sequestered in the back bedroom with Lisa and one of the bridesmaids, to help them dress for the wedding, that the bad mood threatened to return.

It would have been easier if she didn't like Lisa. If Lisa were Kate Peters, Angelle would have had no trouble feeling above it all. But Lisa was friendly and thoughtful, a credit to women everywhere, and when she confessed to

Angelle that she would be needing LaBois consulting services herself, Angelle could feel no anger at all.

"You're getting married?" Angelle asked as casually as she could manage.

"In December. It's kind of sudden, I know. Do you suppose we'll have time to plan a wedding as nice as this one?"

"You'll have to work." And so will I, Angelle thought. I'll have to work hard to put Kyle Sullivan out of my mind.

"I don't care. I'm going to quit my job so I'll have lots of time to take care of details. I want to stay home when we're married anyhow and raise a family."

A family. Kyle's children. Kyle's arms around her at night, Kyle's mouth on hers . . . "I'm delighted for you, Lisa. I hope you'll both be very happy. The two of you deserve it."

There was a moment's hesitation. "Then you know Roy?" Lisa asked tentatively.

"Roy?" Angelle's eyes fastened on Lisa's face. "Roy?"

"Roy Sullivan. I know you and Kyle are friends, but I didn't know you knew Roy."

"Roy?"

Lisa laughed and patted Angelle's flushed cheek. "Kyle's cousin. Roy. My fiancé."

The wedding went off without a hitch. Susan was as beautiful a bride as Angelle had ever clothed. The attendants in their long dresses of lilac and periwinkle were illustrations from a bride's magazine, and the groom and his men were impressively handsome in their gray formal attire. Angelle was certain, beyond the shadow of a doubt, that Kyle Sullivan in a tuxedo was the most wonderful thing she had ever seen.

The reception was held in Susan's church hall, which had been decorated with hundreds of brightly colored balloons. Angelle, alternately thrilled and terror-stricken that Kyle was still available, walked through the reception line in a daze. Kyle was always just out of reach as she mingled with the crowd sampling the wedding buffet. She was still trying to absorb Lisa's news, wondering why she had been so upset anyway, and generally kicking herself, when a Dixieland band began to play.

New Orleanians might have faults, but one thing that no one would ever accuse them of was not knowing how to enjoy themselves. The wedding reception, which might be a sedate occasion in many places, was an excuse to party in a town that really needed no excuses at all.

Angelle found herself dancing with out-of-town uncles, husbands of friends and anyone else who came her way. The music roared around her and the champagne flowed freely. It was a lively, raucous time, and relieved of her depression, she let herself enjoy it thoroughly.

Out of the corner of her eye she saw Kyle dancing with members of the wedding party. When he danced cheek to cheek with Lisa, Angelle didn't even bat an eyelash, but when he finally made his way through the crowd to claim her, she was no longer nonchalant.

Without saying a word, she leaned her head against his white pleated shirt and put her arms around his neck. They swayed to the music, hearts beating in synchronized rhythms. As if they always danced together, they moved in harmony, neither seeming to need a signal as to the other's intentions. They were one body, one entity; united.

"I'm glad you're wearing your hair down, Angel." They were on their second song before Kyle broke the silence.

She was glad he had noticed she had styled it differently the night before. "Do you like it down?"

"It looks like angel hair." He moved his hand up to the back of her neck and wrapped a strand around his finger. "It looks like it should decorate a Christmas tree. It's so soft, so fine."

She couldn't resist. "Do you still think it's not natural?"

He blew along the part that separated the sides of her silvery hair, pretending to examine it carefully. "I might have been wrong."

Angelle threaded one of his curls between her thumb and forefinger and tugged. "Even you can't rile me today."

"It's a most unusual day, then."

"Why do you suppose we irritate each other so much?" The question was lazy, not really searching for deep meaning.

"Are you irritated now?"

"Not at all."

"Neither am I."

"But you are so often. We both are." She ran her fingers down his back to soften her words. "Did you know that normally I'm a very even-tempered person? Angelic, actually."

Kyle bent over and bit her ear, sending rays of feeling sweeping through her body. "I never guessed," he teased. "Did you know that there are actually women in this world who would be flattered by my attentions?"

"I never guessed," she murmured. "Bite my ear again and I'll see if I can figure out why."

He did and she moved closer. "I'll have to admit I'm beginning to see their point."

They finished the dance in silence, each having moved as close as he or she dared.

Finally they stepped apart and joined the applause for the band. "Mrs. Simpson told me about your daughter. I'm very happy for you," Kyle said, not looking at her.

"I wish you had called me. I would have liked to share it with you." She held her breath and waited for his response.

"You made it pretty clear that you didn't want to be in touch, Angel. What was it you said? We weren't compatible. Something about being from two different worlds."

What could she say? That she had changed her mind? She hadn't really. She still thought they were completely different. The truth of the matter was that she no longer had the good sense to make that fact as important as it should be. She wanted to be with Kyle regardless of their differences.

Kyle noticed her long pause and let out an exasperated snort. "Come on, Angel. I'm beyond these little games. We both have people we really care about to share the important details of our lives with. There's no point in pretending, because when it comes down to it, you really have no place for my friendship in your orderly, little-lady existence."

Angelle inclined her head and slapped her hands on her hips. "We're fighting, and you're calling me names again. You don't even give me a chance to form a sentence before you pounce on me!"

"That's just what you need, Angel little lady Reed. Some man to pounce on you. It's time for the little lady to become a little woman. All the genteel discussions and weighted pauses in the world won't cure what ails you."

The musicians were taking a break and the loud roar of conversation had not begun again. Angelle was sure that every person in the crowded room was aware that she and Kyle were fighting. "And you'd like to be the one, wouldn't you, Kyle Sullivan. It's eating you up knowing that you don't have a chance at the job."

"If you think I've been sitting around dreaming about pastel colors, perfume and flowers, you're sadly mistaken."

"No, I imagine you've been contenting yourself with that Amazon phys ed teacher who could probably teach you every game invented by man."

"Your temper is showing, Angel."

"You haven't seen anything yet." And then Angelle Reed, whose reputation in New Orleans society was impeccable,

who clothed the most socially prominent citizens of the city
who had attended the best schools, dated the best men and
been seen in only the best places, kicked Kyle Sullivan in the
shin. "Now you've seen it all," she said sweetly, patting
Kyle on the cheek before she walked away.

First Class Romance

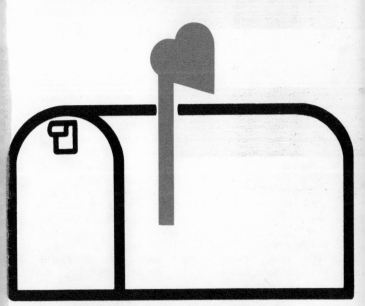

Delivered to your door by
Silhouette Romance®

(See inside for special FREE books and gift offer)

Find romance at your door with 4 FREE novels from Silhouette Romance!

Slip away to a world that's as far away as your mailbox. A world of romance, where the pace of life is as gentle as a kiss, and as fast as the pounding of a lover's heartbeat. Wrap yourself in the special pleasure of having Silhouette Romance novels arrive at your home.

By filling out and mailing the attached postage-paid order card you'll receive—FREE—4 new Silhouette Romance novels (a $7.80 value) plus a FREE Folding Umbrella and Mystery Gift.

You'll also receive an extra bonus: our monthly Silhouette Books Newsletter. Then approximately every 4 weeks we'll send you six more Silhouette Romance novels to examine FREE for 15 days. If you decide to keep them, you'll pay just $11.70, with no extra charge for home delivery and at no risk! You'll also have the option to cancel at any time. Just drop us a note. Your first 4 books, Folding Umbrella and Mystery Gift are yours to keep in any case.

Silhouette Romance ®

A FREE
Folding Umbrella and Mystery Gift await you, too!

CLIP AND MAIL THIS POSTPAID CARD TODAY!

NO POSTAGE
NECESSARY
IF MAILED
IN THE
UNITED STATES

BUSINESS REPLY MAIL
FIRST CLASS PERMIT NO. 194 CLIFTON, N.J.

Postage will be paid by addressee

**Silhouette Books
120 Brighton Road
P.O. Box 5084
Clifton, NJ 07015-9956**

Mail this card today for
4 FREE BOOKS
(a $7.80 value)
and a Folding Umbrella and
Mystery Gift FREE!

Silhouette Romance ®

Silhouette Books, 120 Brighton Rd., P.O. Box 5084, Clifton, NJ 07015-9956

☐ **YES!** Please send me my four SILHOUETTE Romance novels FREE, along with my FREE Folding Umbrella and Mystery Gift, as explained in this insert. I understand that I am under no obligation to purchase any books.

NAME _____
(please print)

ADDRESS _____

CITY _____ STATE _____ ZIP _____

Terms and prices subject to change.
Your enrollment is subject to acceptance by Silhouette Books.

Silhouette Romance is a registered trademark

CMR4X6

Chapter Six

The ECS waiting room was empty when Kyle walked in, finding a seat on the sofa to wait for his appointment with Mrs. Simpson. He stretched his long legs in front of him and folded his arms behind his head. It had been a difficult week with several large construction jobs to oversee. Kyle had driven himself unmercifully. Almost, he thought wryly, as if he had been trying to get away from something.

But there was no getting away from that something here, in this place. Angelle's presence hovered in the sedate waiting room like a cloud of fragrant mist. He had encountered her here so often, watched her converse with others in her warm, well-mannered way, watched her attempts to ignore him. Rarely had she been successful at the latter. From the very beginning they had been drawn together against their wills, almost as if an unseen entity was manipulating them.

Resolutely they had been able to battle the ridiculous though undeniable attraction, and since they would be having no contact in the future, it seemed that they had been permanently successful. Whatever had been blossoming between them would be destroyed for lack of opportunity.

"It's just as well," Kyle muttered, trying to relax. "My shins couldn't stand any more."

Angelle had been enraged at him during the wedding reception, and with chagrin, Kyle knew that she had been right to be. What was it about the silvery-blond Miss Etiquette that made him say such preposterous things, made him act in such preposterous ways? He was still trying to figure it out, eyes tightly closed, when the sofa sagged next to him.

"We have to stop meeting like this," a soft voice whispered in his ear.

"I've thought that was true all along," he said, opening his eyes to stare at Angelle's delicate features. She was dressed in the palest possible pink, and she looked fragile enough to worry about. But Kyle knew that was ridiculous. Tentatively he looked down at her open-toed shoes. "If you kick me with those sandals, you're going to get hurt."

"I'm really sorry about that."

"Where did you learn to pack such a wallop?"

"I grew up with three feisty older brothers. I had to learn to protect myself."

Kyle shut his eyes again. "You're a success."

"I'm not apologizing for kicking you, only for doing it in front of half of New Orleans."

"I'm sorry too, Angel, but you make me say the most outrageous things."

"I make you say them? How can you pretend that I . . ."

"Oh, I don't think you try to. Not really. But we rub each other the wrong way. You think I'm a big, uncouth football player with pigskin between my ears. I think you're a . . ."

Angelle was leaning forward, her blue eyes snapping. "You think I'm what?"

"I think you're very angry. And if this continues, we might just stage another scene like the last one, only this time with Mrs. Simpson present."

Angelle was instantly contrite. "You make me say the most outrageous things."

"I make you? How can you pretend that I—"

"Angelle, Kyle?" Mrs. Simpson was standing beside the sofa. "Are you ready?"

Kyle opened his eyes and stood up quickly. "Did you want to see us together?"

Mrs. Simpson nodded, her face showing no emotion. "It concerns you both."

Without a word they followed her into her office, not daring to look at each other. Mrs. Simpson motioned them to take seats in front of her desk.

Angelle was distinctly uncomfortable. She had spent the past week trying to forget Kyle existed, and she had begun to believe that she was succeeding. Now she was back in his presence and well aware that she had been deluding herself. If she moved halfway around the globe and never encountered him again, she might be able to put him out of her mind. But seeing him time and time again with weeks in between was like watching a film that used time-lapse photography to chronicle the growth of a flower from a seed to an unfolded blossom. Her feelings were growing and that growth was clearly apparent every time she saw him.

"Well, I'm afraid I have some very bad news for both of you." Mrs. Simpson was not looking directly at either of them; she was pushing several pieces of paper around her desk. "I'm going to have to place the children I spoke to you about in another home."

Kyle and Angelle gasped simultaneously. "Why?"

Finally Mrs. Simpson lifted her head. "This is probably hard to understand, but so many things can go wrong between here and Korea. We knew that the children needed families, and every bit of information we had on them convinced us that making them legally available for adoption wouldn't be difficult. What we didn't know, and what we just discovered, is that your children are brother and sister."

"You're kidding." Angelle shook her head. "And no one knew?"

"The orphanage staff knew, but the woman who translated for me when I visited didn't make it clear. Her English was very difficult to understand, and I thought she was saying that the children were good friends. Their records are unbelievably scanty. They didn't even include the children's surnames or that would have been a clue. Anyhow, the woman who coordinates our adoptions in Korea wasn't told until early this week. You see, the children came into the orphanage at different times because the little girl, Jin Ah, was in a hospital for a while. I noticed that Young Ki paid her special attention, but I thought he just felt sorry for her. Of course when the legal work was begun, the truth came out."

"And they can't be adopted because they're siblings?" Kyle asked with a frown.

"They can't be adopted by two different parents. I don't want them separated."

There was a long silence. "Do you ever place siblings in separate homes?" Angelle asked finally.

Mrs. Simpson nodded. "Occasionally it's done. And to be honest, I'd do it this time without blinking an eye. It's going to take precious time to find another family, and I want those children in this country where Jin Ah can get the medical attention she needs. But . . ." Her voice trailed off.

"But," Kyle prodded.

"But I can't place them with you and Angelle." Mrs. Simpson was obviously struggling with the words to convey her decision. "If I thought that the two of you would make an honest effort to let the children spend quantities of time together, I'd go ahead as planned. But I'd have to be blind not to have seen the tension between you. From the very beginning, you've been at each other's throat.''

Angelle could feel the color rising in her cheeks. She wanted to protest, but she couldn't. She glanced at Kyle and saw him gripping the arms of his chair.

"And so," Mrs. Simpson went on, "I'm going to have to put this adoption on hold until I have another family who is willing to take them both. I'm sorry, I hate to do it.''

"I'd take them both in a minute," Angelle declared.

"That's straining your resources too far, too fast," Mrs. Simpson chided her. "We have to think of the children.''

"I think you've misread the situation," Kyle said finally in a calm voice. "Angelle and I would never let anything stand between those children and happiness. We're both firmly rooted in New Orleans with no plans to leave, and we'd make every effort to be sure the children grew up together.''

Angelle was nodding eagerly. "Kyle's right," she said.

But Mrs. Simpson was shaking her head. "I know you're both terribly disappointed. I've searched my mind for one sign that the two of you could work this out, but I couldn't think of anything.''

Angelle could feel happiness slipping out of her grasp. As surely as if she had carried Jin Ah inside her for nine months, the little girl was hers. Jin Ah was firmly rooted in her heart. So Angelle, who prided herself on doing the socially acceptable, who considered herself above reproach in her personal and professional life, told the first lie of her adulthood.

"Well, would you see the fact that Kyle is moving into the other half of my house as a sign?''

Mrs. Simpson frowned, and Angelle was afraid to see what Kyle was doing. She hurried on. "Kyle and I have talked at great length about the need for our kids to have someone familiar in their lives. When my tenants moved out, Kyle volunteered to move in. It's not a permanent arrangement, but we felt sure that it would be good for the kids at first. We didn't even know they were brother and sister." She waited for lightning to strike or Kyle to choke.

"I knew nothing about this," Mrs. Simpson said. Angelle wondered if the social worker really believed her.

Kyle answered. "We just decided. I was going to tell you today."

Angelle was bathed in relief; he was not going to refute her story. "Kyle and I have actually become good friends," she added eagerly. "We both thought it would be very supportive to be next door to each other during those initial trying days." Good friends? The lies were getting more and more unbelievable. Kyle's arm had somehow found its way across the back of her chair, and he pinched the nape of her neck in warning.

"Both of you know, don't you, that we have to think of the children's future before we consider anything else?"

Kyle and Angelle both nodded solemnly.

"And you do understand that their best interests might not be yours—"

"I think all our interests are the same," Kyle interrupted. "Those children will be very lucky to have us as parents, and we'll be very lucky to have them. Angelle and I would never let personal differences stand in their way. You'll be doing us all a disservice if you decide otherwise."

Mrs. Simpson gazed thoughtfully at them. "Frankly, I'm not sure what to do," she finally conceded. "I'm going to have to give it some thought." She stood. "I'll let you know my decision. In the meantime, we'll continue doing the necessary paperwork until I decide otherwise." She stood and held out her hand to Angelle. "If this doesn't work out, there will be other children for both of you."

"Jin Ah is my child," Angelle said firmly.

"Young Ki is mine," Kyle echoed.

"Believe me, I'll give it every consideration," Mrs. Simpson said. "I'll be calling to let you know."

"Just tell me one thing," Kyle said when he and Angelle were on the elevator inching their way to the first floor. "Is the other side of your apartment painted pink too?"

"It's white," Angelle answered tonelessly.

"Thank God." They stood side by side in total silence for the long minutes that it took the elevator to deposit them at their destination.

"Kyle," Angelle started when they were standing in the hall, "I'm so sorry I got you into this."

Kyle put his fingers under her chin and lifted her face to meet his eyes. "I was just thinking how I've misjudged you."

She was confused. "I don't understand."

"Let's find a place to talk. How about the coffee shop?"

Angelle made an involuntary face. "If you're not in a hurry, we could go to my place. I could even show you the apartment."

"Sounds good. I'll meet you there in a half an hour."

He didn't seem angry. Angelle wasn't sure what he was feeling, but there was at least a small ray of hope that the afternoon could go by without a major battle between them. With that one positive thought to tide her over, she went to get her car.

Angelle had just taken out cheese and crackers and set them on the coffee table when her doorbell rang. She straightened sofa cushions on her way to the door. "Hi, come on in."

Kyle looked especially rugged, she thought as she gestured him inside. The weather was beginning to take on a slight chill, and he had compensated by wearing rust corduroy slacks and a lightweight cream sweater. The wind had ruffled his reddish curls, and there was a sunburned patch on his nose. He looked like the appealing Irishman he was.

"Have a seat," she said, gesturing to the sofa. "Can I get you something to drink?"

"I'll take a beer if you have it."

She nodded and went to the kitchen, returning with beer in a frosted mug. She sat next to him, sipping the wine she had poured herself.

"Well?" she said finally.

"Angelle, you're a trooper." Kyle shifted his weight and turned to face her. "I would never in a million years have thought you were capable of coming up with such a brilliant solution to our mutual predicament."

"Thanks a lot." She set her wine down with a bang. "So you didn't think I was capable of having an intelligent idea, huh? That figures."

Kyle tried again. "Not at all. What I didn't think you were capable of was rescuing us both simultaneously. And frankly, I didn't think you'd ever even want to help me out."

She shrugged, picking up the wineglass and twirling it between her palms. "Kyle, in this case what's good for one of us is good for us both. I'm just glad you were willing to go along with it."

"I'd do anything I had to in order to convince Mrs. Simpson that Young Ki belongs with me."

"Even live in my house?"

"Live in your house, mow your lawn, eat your cooking," he couldn't resist, "sleep in your bed . . ."

Angelle sniffed. "That's not part of the arrangement."

"Too bad—what's good for one of us could be good for us both," he said, restating her earlier words.

"Are you trying to ruin this already?" She shook her head. "That's just exactly the kind of thing that gets us in trouble every time. You can't keep from trying to get under my skin."

"Well said."

Angelle hit the sofa between them with a bang. "Stop it right now, Kyle. If this keeps up we'll both lose our kids. Learning to get along is the price we'll have to pay to become parents."

"It's been that way through the ages. First a couple learns to get along, then the children come . . . What could be simpler." Kyle dodged the pillow that Angelle hurled at him.

"You're impossible. An Irish moron. A Gaelic barbarian."

"A man willing to go along with your plans."

Angelle stopped her tirade. "You promise?"

"I promise."

"Boy, this is going to take some getting used to."

"I suggest we start tonight." Kyle set his empty beer mug on the coffee table, grinning as Angelle lifted the dripping mug and slid a coaster beneath. "Let's spend the evening together getting to know each other."

Coming from Kyle, the offer was too suspicious. "Doing what?" she asked.

"There's never a scarcity of possibilities in this town. Let's go out for dinner, poke around the French Quarter, listen to music. I don't care."

Having expected him to make a pass at her, she was almost disappointed his plans were so pure. To cover up her feelings, she nodded with false enthusiasm. "All right."

"What shall it be—dinner, the Quarter, or music?"

"Yes," Angelle decided. "Let's do it all."

She insisted they go dutch treat and he relented, grumbling about little-lady liberation. While Angelle combed her hair and freshened up, Kyle toured his new home.

"It's not too bad," he told Angelle when she was ready. "I can manage for a while."

"I'm glad. Somehow I can't really imagine you here; I appreciate your going along with the move."

"I'm looking for a house to buy. Something with a good-sized yard and room for Young Ki to grow in. This will be all right for a start, though."

Kyle, the Saint, a domesticated animal. It was hard to picture. Angelle locked the house behind her and then turned, spying the red Volvo station wagon in front of her house. "Is that yours? I thought you borrowed it for the wedding."

"All mine." He walked around the front of the car and opened the door for her. "Did you think I went everywhere on the cycle?"

She nodded.

"Even football players get cold in the winter. Besides, motorcycles are dangerous for children." He walked around the car and slid underneath the steering wheel. "Where would you like to eat?"

"I'm not very hungry." The afternoon's events had taken away her appetite. "Let's eat something simple in the Quarter."

"Have you been to the Jax Brewery yet?"

The Jackson Brewery had been a New Orleans landmark for almost one hundred years. The nineteenth-century brew house had shut down its plant on Decatur Street in the French Quarter a decade before, but the building had recently undergone a fifteen-million-dollar renovation, turning it into a specialty marketplace. Angelle hadn't had a chance yet to visit.

With Angelle's enthusiastic consent, Kyle parked on a French Quarter side street. The Quarter, as it was called by local residents, was the original New Orleans, more Spanish in architecture than French, but still named after the first settlers. Kyle took her arm, and they walked through the narrow streets under iron lace balconies, many decorated with forests of hanging plants.

At Jackson Square they crossed Decatur Street and turned toward the brewery, admiring the castlelike structure with its tasteful gray trimmed in dark red with outsize copper drainpipes. Inside Kyle casually took Angelle's hand to keep from being separated in the crowd that filled the building to overflowing. Hand in hand they wandered through the first- and second-floor specialty shops, deciding when they tired to forego any of the sit-down restaurants for the more informal fare offered in the third-floor Jaxfest.

Jaxfest was a conglomeration of New Orleans' eating experiences served from booths and kiosks. Armed with cannola, oysters, fried chicken, potato salad and pecan pie, they found their way to a marble table on one of the terraces behind the building that looked over the mighty Mississippi.

"Oh, I like this," Angelle crowed. "It opens up the riverfront." She sat gazing across the water as she munched on fried chicken. "We sing about her, we drink her, we have a real love affair with her, but we hardly ever get to just enjoy her. This is terrific."

"Her?"

"The Mississippi. Don't you know the river is female?"

"What makes you think so? What ever happened to 'Old Man River'...?" Kyle popped a fried oyster into his mouth and licked his fingers.

"She's the giver of life, the nurturer; she's strong and sure, but she can rock her children gently when they need it."

"Or she can flood the land with the fury of a woman scorned."

"That too." Angelle took a bite of the cannola and offered the rest of it to Kyle. "You don't like women very much, do you?"

He ate the cannola right out of her hand. "Not very much. My experiences haven't been the best."

She watched his tongue come out to lick the remainder of the ricotta-filled Italian pastry off her fingers. The sensation was more sensual than she could have guessed it would be, and when he was finished she stroked his cheek. "I'm sorry they haven't been. Your ex-wife must have been crazy."

Now what had made her say that? The poor woman was probably a saint to have married Kyle Sullivan in the first place.

"Dale was no more or no less than I knew she was when I married her."

"Then why did you marry her?"

There was a long pause as Kyle considered the question. "Let's just say that she was all the woman I thought I could handle."

It was a curious answer, but Angelle decided it was all the answer that she could handle. Still, she couldn't resist a final word on the subject. "My grandmother always says that when you expect nothing, you get nothing."

"Does that apply to you as well?"

She had never thought about it, but perhaps it did. She hadn't made a mistake as Kyle had with Dale. She hadn't made any mistakes at all. Yet, it was hard to admit. "I think it's a little different for me," she hedged. "It's not really that I expect nothing, it's more that I want nothing. I'm happy without a man in my life."

"There's a whole dimension of your life missing."

There was a cool breeze blowing, and the sun was just beginning to set, turning the sky behind them into a radiant canopy. Kyle's remark would normally have made her angry, but there, with the Mississippi rolling in front of them, and the air around them cooling into color-saturated mist, there was no room for anger. And too, Kyle was exactly right.

"Yes, and I can't really pretend that I want it that way," she said quietly.

His hand came around her to rest on her spine. "Don't tell me you haven't had any chances."

"Chances for what, Kyle? To go to bed with a stranger who wants a one-night romp and no responsibility? Chances to marry a decent man who would give me stability and undying affection? I've had plenty of chances, all along the spectrum of chances, but never a chance I wanted to take."

"And so we see another in the long series of differences between us." His hand began a slow, sensual assault along her spine, finally ending at the back of her neck where he began to massage the tense muscles he found. "My standards were so low that I settled for too little, and your standards are so high that you won't settle for anything."

She nodded her head, pleasure flooding her body at his careful touch. "We should average our standards, merge our expectations. Maybe both of us would be better adjusted for it."

"Merge? The idea is appealing."

Angelle snorted. "In any kind of merger with you, Kyle Sullivan, I'd be the loser. You wouldn't merge, you'd swallow me alive."

"I've never met a woman who was a less likely candidate for boa constrictor bait, Angel. You may worry about losing your identity if you ever give yourself to a man, but I don't think there's any real reason for concern."

A casual intimacy had risen between them, binding them with warm feelings and reluctant admiration for each other. "This is nice, isn't it?" Angelle said, leaning toward Kyle and laying her head on his shoulder. "I like being with you when we don't fight." She felt a moist pressure on the top of her head and a sensation of warmth radiated through her body. If she hadn't known that displays of genuine affection were foreign to their relationship, she would have sworn that Kyle had just kissed her.

Some places are magic, and Angelle, who had grown up in New Orleans, had always been sure that the French Quarter was one of them. With Kyle by her side, walking through the narrow streets, examining shop windows and watching the people they passed took on a magic all its own. They seldom touched or talked, but they were curiously in tune as they wandered down Royal Street and finally to Bourbon.

"Do you mind?" Kyle asked nodding his head at one of the more seamy nightspots on the street.

"I'm not made of spun glass. I won't shatter if I walk by. Just hold my hand so that dingy little man doesn't pull me in the front door."

"And should I cover your eyes as well to keep you from gawking at the strip show in there?"

She smiled. "Next you'll offer to stand in front of me to bar my view while you look your fill."

Holding hands, they continued down the middle of the street, which was closed to traffic. Kyle pointed down a side street. "I've got friends who play at a place around that corner. Would you like to sit and listen for a while?"

It was still early, and Angelle was in no hurry for the evening to end. She was curious to see how long they could sustain the truce between them. It had been exactly two hours and forty-five minutes since they had argued. "I'd like that."

There were plenty of places to sit since the evening was still young by Bourbon Street standards. Kyle led Angelle to a table close to the front. Immediately two of the musicians, who were between sets, came over to greet them.

After affectionate exchanges between the men, and the introduction of Angelle to the band—all of whom finally made their way to the table—the music began. And what glorious music it was. New Orleans jazz, smoky, rasping heartbreaking jazz. Music meant to chill the listener to the bone, to warm him to fever pitch, to melt, to freeze, to draw out his soul. Angelle was caught in its spell, completely lost.

She was unaware when Kyle ordered drinks for them; she was unaware when he moved his chair closer to her and covered her hand with his. Was it the music that was flooding her with feelings long denied? The music that cut through her polite veneer and exposed the woman inside? She found that she could scarcely breathe, scarcely move. When she realized Kyle was so close, she was grateful for his presence, grateful for his warmth.

The band ended the long set with "Oh When the Saints," and dedicated it to Kyle. When they were done, Angelle found herself coming back to reality slowly. Her drink was gone, and her head was pillowed on Kyle's chest.

"You really get into that, don't you, Angel? I never would have guessed."

She traced the pattern of reddish hair on the back of his hands. Fine, strong hands with callused fingertips. Capable hands that could give pleasure. Hands to hold a woman until she knew, was sure, that she had been held.

What was she thinking? "It's in my blood, just as it's in yours," she whispered. What, she wondered, was she really referring to? The music? Or something else, something more primitive that had been released by the squalling, pulsating sounds.

That the music was in Kyle's blood became evident during the next set. After the third song, the trumpeter stepped up to the mike and asked Kyle to come play with them. Angelle was shaken out of her reverie by the news that Kyle was a musician. It seemed impossible, incongruous, but it was true. And what a musician. Another trumpet was passed to Kyle and he began to play, at first as just a member of the ensemble, but as the song progressed and each instrument took its turn doing a solo, his time came.

Each note was crystal clear and haunting. A wailing sound that blew straight into Angelle's body, filling it with pressure, steady aching pressure that only increased with each new note. Kyle turned to her as he played, stepping forward to send the music crashing past her, crashing through her, as if he knew just what he was doing. She was enchanted, entranced, sitting at the table with her lips softly parted as if she was beseeching him to continue. When he finally stopped, there was loud applause, but Angelle was completely oblivious to anything except Kyle and the pleasure he had given her.

It was very late when they walked back to the car. There was very little to say, and they moved as one with arms wrapped tightly around each other's waist. It had been exactly five hours and ten minutes since they had fought.

Kyle pulled up in front of Angelle's house and came around to help her out of the car. They walked up the front steps together, but the spell was beginning to dissolve.

"Would you like to come in for a drink before you go?" she asked shyly. She didn't want to see the evening end, even though it had to.

"I think, Angel, that coming in would not be a good idea."

He was right, but still there had to be a more fitting conclusion than a casual goodbye. "It's been a very special evening, Kyle." Trying to put it on a businesslike basis, she added, "I'm sure now that you and I can get along well enough to pull off this living arrangement."

Kyle framed her face with his hands. "I don't think that's going to be the problem, little lady."

The nickname was a caress. In anticipation and in dread, Angelle shut her eyes. "I could pretend that I don't know what you mean...."

Kyle's mouth when it met hers was like the music he had played for her. The passion devoured her, swept inside her to fill her with needs, with desires she couldn't express, couldn't admit to. His hands tangled in her hair and then caressed her back, pulling her closer and finally reaching lower to lift her against him. "You're so little. I'm afraid you'll shatter when I hold you, like a crystal angel on a Christmas tree."

"Little but not fragile," she said before he kissed her again. She opened her mouth with no prodding, seeking the warmth of his first. Kyle's arm tightened around her, and she could feel the buttons of his shirt beneath the light sweater he wore. Finally she pulled her mouth from his, resting her head against his chest as she listened to his heart beat.

"What am I going to do with you, Angel?"

The answer seemed simple enough, but the simple answer was not the right answer in this case. "You're going to say good-night and go home," she said instead. "And you are going to go to bed, wake up in the morning and realize how foolish this is."

"I already realize that. But I seem to be powerless to stop it from happening."

"It's just chemistry. Hormones," she said, trying to be practical, and pulling away completely from his embrace as she did. "We're just so geared up to fight that when we can't, we don't know what else to do."

"Another way to look at it is that we're so geared up for something else that when we deny ourselves, we fight instead."

"My version is easier to live with," Angelle said with a firmness she didn't feel.

"For whom?"

"For both of us. We'd be crazy to let ourselves get carried away. Too much is at stake here, and I don't intend to lose any of it just because we can't control ourselves."

"Then you'll have to try to stop seducing me, Angel."

She blinked, not believing what she had just heard. "Seducing you! You big..." She focused on Kyle's grin and realized what he was trying to do. Against her will she flashed her dimples at him. "Nice try, macho man, but it's not going to work. I'm not going to fight with you tonight."

"You know what that means then, don't you?" Without another word, he pulled her close, running the palms of his hands down her back to rest on her bottom, lifting her as he did. The kiss was restrained. It was a whisper that before had been a war cry. He savored what before he had devoured.

"Good night, Kyle," she murmured against his mouth, slipping down again at the end of the kiss. "I'll see you soon."

When she was safely inside, she stood with her back braced against the door. Whether she was trying to keep someone in or someone out of the little shotgun house, she wasn't sure at all.

Chapter Seven

Angelle was lying in a field of wild flowers, wearing a patterned dress fashioned from yards and yards of sheer organdy. Beside her lay a wide-brimmed, picture-book hat decorated with pastel satin ribbons. On the other side of her lay a man she obviously cared about, judging from the position of his arm, which was draped comfortably across her breast. There were wispy summer clouds overhead, and with utmost contentment she was watching them drift across the deep blue of the sky.

It was a glorious day. The sunshine was golden. The flowers beneath her felt like a velvet carpet. The man beside her was warm and enticing. Angelle was sure the perfect moment would never end.

But as she watched, the clouds began to take shapes and to descend closer and closer—white, smothering masses of cotton fluff. She was paralyzed, unable to even shut her eyes to avoid watching their suffocating approach. Then they were covering her face, choking off the very air she was trying desperately to inhale.

She shrieked, using every ounce of her strength to sit up and push the clouds, which felt warm and silky to the touch, away from her face. A terrified mewing sound brought her sharply awake. She was sitting up in her bed, and Miaou was trying desperately to climb up her nightgown to regain her tenuous perch on Angelle's head.

Angelle peeled the distraught cat off the now-shredded negligee, wincing as claws caught the skin of her shoulder. "You dumb cat! You scared me to death. What were you doing sleeping on my face?"

Miaou was oblivious to her mistress's voice, continuing to flail as Angelle held her firmly away. "Watch it, or I'll feed you to that dog I hear barking next door!"

Dog barking next door? She dropped the cat unceremoniously on the bed where it promptly climbed to the top of the French Provincial headboard and froze. Grabbing the robe that matched the ruined negligee, Angelle threw it on and ran barefoot to the window, just in time to see four of the largest men the world had ever known carrying a sofa up her front walk. Kyle was behind them singlehandedly managing a matching armchair. Behind Kyle romped his two golden retrievers.

It was moving day. A week had passed. Kyle Sullivan was coming to live in her house. Without thinking, she knocked on the window to get his attention and lifted her arm to wave. It was only in the split second before he raised his head that she realized that she might as well not be wearing anything. The negligee and robe were a peach-colored chiffon that was so diaphanous that when the set had been unpacked at the bridal shop, Maw Maw had refused to put it on display. In defiance of her own tendency to wear angel costumes, Angelle had spirited it away for herself.

"Good God." Without waiting to see the big smile that was surely covering Kyle's face, she ran back to her bedroom to find something more appropriate to put on. Hastily she pulled on her wheat-colored jeans and a violet shirt, stopping only to run a brush through her hair and a washcloth over her face.

She dashed back to the front of the house in time to see Kyle and his four bulky moving men coming up the front walk carrying a piano. "Can I help?" she asked inanely.

"Coffee," Kyle grunted. "Lots of it."

She filled her biggest coffeepot with New Orleans coffee with chicory, and when it was ready, she poured it into a thermos and made another pot. The night before she had baked several loaves of pumpkin bread, telling herself sternly that she would freeze them for Thanksgiving dinner. Now she sliced them, as she had intended all along, and heaped the thick slices on a platter for Kyle and his friends.

By the time she was finished, the piano had been set in a place of honor in Kyle's living room, and the five movers were strewn over his long expanse of cypress floor. "Would anyone care for some coffee and pumpkin bread?" she asked, poking her head through the connecting door.

Two loaves of pumpkin bread and twelve cups of coffee later, Angelle had met all the men. One of them was an ex-football player like Kyle, one was Kyle's cousin Roy, Lisa's fiancé, and the other two worked for Kyle's construction firm. The little house reeked of good honest sweat and masculinity. The men teased her about her poor judgment in choosing Kyle as her tenant, and then they teased Kyle about his good luck.

The dogs cavorted through the house sniffing out each new smell directly under the feet of the men who made trip after trip to the rental moving van to bring more furniture and boxes into the house. Finally everything was inside, and with a wave and a reminder to Kyle that he had promised them a keg of beer and a party as soon as he was unpacked and settled, his friends piled into the van and drove off.

Angelle had retreated to her own side of the house after saying goodbye, and she had just finished washing coffee cups when she heard Kyle open the connecting door in the living room. Her kitchen was a perfectly adequate size, larger than most kitchens in modern tract houses, but when Kyle came in to stand behind her, it felt like a room in a dollhouse. She turned and leaned against the sink as she dried the last cup. "So, everything's unloaded."

They hadn't been alone since their night together in the French Quarter. They had discussed moving arrangements on the telephone, and once she'd seen him at a distance in Audubon Park. Having him so close, however, was very, very different. He was smiling at her, and her toes were trying to curl in response. She almost missed his polite reply. "Everything. But I think I'll be unpacking for weeks."

"It's going to be hard for you to find anything to cook with tonight. Why don't I make dinner for you?" Where had that invitation come from? In the week that they had been apart, she had organized her thoughts on the matter of Kyle Sullivan. The new living arrangement would not change anything except their probability of adopting two small children. Religiously she had repeated five simple words to herself every night. "I will not get involved."

"That's a very neighborly gesture." His eyes were crinkling with suppressed laughter, and she knew her internal monologue was blatantly apparent.

"We New Orleanians are nothing if not polite." She turned and opened the overhead cabinet door, pulling a footstool over in order to reach the shelf for the cups.

"Let me." In a second he was beside her, taking the fragile china from her hands to place it on the shelf. With Angelle standing on the footstool they were eye to eye. "How does it feel to be my size?" he asked. Their faces were almost touching.

"It's certainly a different perspective."

She was sure Kyle was going to kiss her; she could almost taste him against her lips, when a screech from the other room brought them both up short.

"What in the hell?"

"Miaou!"

"That was more than just a simple meow." Kyle charged through the door followed closely by Angelle. In the pileup of rooms that was unique to the shotgun house, the next room was Angelle's bedroom. There, with her back arched, they found Miaou, claws extended, preparing to jump from the headboard of Angelle's bed onto the back of one of the retrievers.

"Gipper, get away." The retriever had its front paws on the bed—more correctly on Angelle's shredded negligee, which she had thrown forgotten on top of the sheets when she had dressed so hurriedly.

The dog obeyed with obvious canine reluctance, swiveling to put all four paws on the floor. One long doggie toenail brought the negligee to the floor too.

"It's all right, Miaou," Angelle soothed, not daring to get too close to the cat's unsheathed claws herself. "What would the dogs do to her if they caught her?" she asked Kyle, turning to find him holding the tattered negligee up to the light, his forehead wrinkled in a frown.

"Have you been entertaining King Kong in this, Angel?"

"Give me that." She grabbed for the diaphanous flesh-colored chiffon, but he held it out of reach.

"I can see how this would drive a man crazy, but I'm surprised you survived his attentions."

"Kyle, I'm warning you, give me that."

He shook his head in mock regret. "And I was so sure of your purity, little lady. Woe is me, led astray again by a pretty face." He covered his eyes with one hand as he handed her the gown. "Is there not a chaste woman left in the universe?"

"Cut out the dramatics, you big oaf. The cat ripped it to shreds when she heard your dogs this morning."

"A likely story."

She opened her mouth to bellow something appropriately vicious at him when she realized that he was laughing at her.

"As for the dogs, no, they wouldn't hurt the cat. They just want to play with her. They're really very gentle, big hulks that they are. If she'll just stop spitting fire at them and cozy up, they'll treat her like the little lady she is." His hand reached up to caress the velvet skin under Angelle's chin. "Sound familiar? It's an allegory."

"I'll see you for dinner at seven." She couldn't help it; she had to smile at him. "What do you like?"

"If your pumpkin bread is a clue, I'll like anything you fix, Angel." He walked to the door, a hand on the collar of each dog. "By the way, is it too much to ask you to model that negligee for me again?"

He was gone, and she could hear the connecting door in the living room slam before she could think of an answer.

She settled on shrimp *étouffée*, a seafood concoction cooked in a savory sauce, served on rice. And she decided to double her usual recipe. Kyle hadn't grown up to be a football player eating dainty portions; she wanted to be prepared. She fixed a large tossed salad and bought a yard-long loaf of fresh French bread. For dessert she visited the neighborhood bakery and bought two chocolate éclairs.

She knew it wasn't necessary to change, but after taking off her jeans to get into the shower, she decided not to put them back on. Instead she slipped into a skirt and blouse of darkest cranberry and found sheer patterned hose to match.

The rich color made her hair seem even lighter, and she tied a cranberry ribbon around her face to heighten the effect. She liked what she saw, although Kyle might not recognize her out of her usual pastels.

She was putting the finishing touches on the table when she heard Kyle's knock. "Come in," she called. The connecting door was still unlocked, a fact that had never been true when she had rented to other tenants, and she made a mental note to lock it after Kyle left that night. There was no point in asking for trouble.

Kyle had changed too. He was wearing a rust-colored sports jacket and an ivory shirt with the mandatory three buttons unfastened. His hair was still damp from the recent shower she had heard him taking through the thin walls separating the two apartments. It had been a strange experience to know that as she was standing in her own bathroom brushing her hair, Kyle was only a few feet away standing naked under gallons of warm water, getting ready to eat dinner with her. She had finished brushing her hair in her bedroom.

"Something smells spectacular." He held out his arms and she noticed for the first time that they were filled with roses. "I brought you something."

"They're lovely," she stammered, completely unstrung by the courtesy. Roses from Kyle?

"They're from my garden."

"Your garden?" She found a vase in a cabinet beneath the sink and filled it with water, bringing it over to the table.

"The house I rented on Henry Clay had an old abandoned rose garden when I moved in. I took it over, saved most of the old bushes and planted some new ones. It was the only thing about the house that I hated to leave, but the new tenants have promised to take good care of it."

The sentimentality of the statement was a surprise. "I can't imagine you growing roses," she said with a teasing flash of her dimples. "I'd expect some sort of hefty vegetable—you know, beefsteak tomatoes, Big Max pumpkins, Macho melons."

"Macho melons?"

"I made that one up," she admitted.

"Are you a gardener?" he asked. "I noticed how well kept your backyard is. Actually, I found the size of the yard amazing. How did you come by all that space?"

"This was the key lot originally. You should be thankful too. Now the dogs have a place to run."

"Then you don't mind if I put them out there?"

She finished arranging the roses and stepped back to admire her handiwork. "No, I don't mind. Everything that's planted back there is very sturdy. My brother John helped my brother Charles landscape originally, and Charles absolutely insisted on maintenance-free shrubbery."

"The house is a family affair, then?"

"Everything in my life is a family affair. When they noticed that I was growing up, my brothers just took over my life. They decided I should buy this house from Charles, that I should help my grandmother at LaBois Bridal, and that I should meet and marry the right man." She bit her tongue at reciting the last item on the list.

"Did you mind?"

"Only the latter. The house and the job were my ideas too, even though they didn't notice, but they're appalled at how stubborn I've been about their marriage plans for me." She tried for a change of subject. "Would you like some wine before dinner? It will be a few more minutes."

He followed her through her bedroom and sitting room into the living room. When they were comfortably settled on the sofa he reopened their dialogue. "So tell me about these so-called attempts to marry you off."

The sofa was really no more than a love seat, and Angelle, who had been trying to put emotional distance between herself and Kyle all day, found that any sort of distance was going to be impossible. "Well, there's nothing very interesting to report. My father moved to Miami the year I graduated from college, and my brothers decided that with Daddy so far away, they had to be responsible for me. You know all about the Southern chivalric code, I'm sure. None of them really had the time to hover over me the way they thought they should, so they began to attempt, in earnest, to find me a husband."

"But you wouldn't go along with their plans." Kyle shifted in his place, brushing her leg with his. It was the first time he had touched her all evening, and she had to stop for a moment to gather her wits about her again.

"No, I wouldn't," she finally continued. "They did the most ridiculous things. One of my brothers joined a carnival social club that parades for Mardi Gras, just to keep his eye open for eligible bachelors for me. Another one, Charles, made sure that all the single men who came to his office looking for houses to buy were referred to him. John, the landscaper, tried to get me interested in joining the New Orleans cactus growers organization because he heard that most of the members were male."

Kyle was shaking with laughter, and Angelle couldn't help smiling either, although at the time her brother's plotting hadn't been funny at all. "Were they blind?" he asked finally. "All they had to do was take a good look at you. I'm sure every eligible bachelor in New Orleans has his eye on you already."

She experienced a rush of pleasure at the strange compliment. "Actually," she said, "when it comes to me, they are blind. They still see me as little A.C., their tagalong kid sister who could never throw a football as well as they could or steal home when they told her to."

"I begin to see why you're not crazy about men."

Angelle thought the statement might be amended to "some men, Kyle Sullivan not included," but instead she said, "Let's eat."

"Do they still check up on you?" Kyle asked over the *étouffée*.

"Twice a week, like clockwork, one of them calls on some pretense or the other. I think they have a rotation worked out."

"Do you see them often?"

Angelle smiled, passing him the French bread as she said, "They're really quite sweet. I like their wives, and among them they've given me nine terrific nephews, so I see them as much as I can. I don't like their meddling, but I like them."

"And do they like you?"

She stopped, fork halfway to her mouth to ponder his question. "I really don't know. Do men ever like women?"

"I'm not sure what you mean." Kyle broke off another piece of French bread and sat back in his chair to eat it.

"Well, in my experience, men desire me, or they want to protect me or even control me, but I don't think that ever, in my whole life, have I met a man who really liked me. I can't speak for my entire sex, but I think that real friendship between a man and a woman is rarer than a cool day in August."

"There are a lot of good marriages out there based on friendship as well as desire." Kyle looked up and his face was almost bashful. "Now that's a statement, coming from me."

"Yes, it has to be the first positive thing to come out of your mouth about marriage," Angelle said with a dimple. "Could it be that the hard-hearted Kyle Sullivan really secretly believes in happily ever after?"

"Happily ever after is for fairy tales, but I've seen a couple of good marriages up close. And I've seen what happens when they end." He stood up as if to stop the conversation, and began to clear off his place, taking his plate to the sink. "Shall I wash or dry?"

"Don't bother with either. Let's have coffee and dessert in the living room." She gave him the plate with the éclairs on it and watched as he took it into the living room. What had he meant by his last cryptic remark? Was he thinking of his own failed marriage? She doubted that, because Kyle had made it sound as though his own marriage had never been good. No, he was obviously referring to some other event in his life, some other relationship that had ended painfully. Angelle wanted to ask him, but he had made it clear that the subject was closed. Somehow she knew that if she could understand his words, a large portion of the mystery of Kyle Sullivan would be unlocked forever.

"Well, do you think you'll be comfortable living here?" Angelle asked as they sat together eating the éclairs.

"I'm always amazed at just how roomy these crazy houses are. Everything fit nicely and I still have an empty room for Young Ki."

"If Young Ki comes." They sat in silence for a while, sipping the coffee. "You haven't heard anything from Mrs. Simpson, have you?" Angelle asked finally. "I haven't heard a word myself."

"No, I've gone ahead with the paperwork as she suggested, though. I'm trying to be optimistic."

"So am I. I've been fingerprinted, notarized, authenticated, researched in triplicate. It's going to be hard to accept if Mrs. Simpson still decides that we can't adopt the children."

"I bought a book of Korean phrases yesterday. I'm going to try and memorize as many as I can." Kyle stretched his arm along the back of the sofa, grazing Angelle's hair.

"I bought a book on child development so that I'll know what to expect from a three-year-old." Ever so slightly, she leaned her head on his arm. The position was very cozy.

"Would you like to practice the Korean together?" Kyle curled his arm to rest his hand lightly on her shoulder.

She nodded, turning so that her cheek was on his arm and her eyes were on his face. "Yes. Would you like me to check out the development of five-year-old boys?"

His eyes glistened. "Yes, and how about thirty-two-year-old men while you're at it."

Her eyes drifted shut as he closed the distance to kiss her. For once, there wasn't an ounce of fight in her. Gone were all her good intentions, her decision to resist him. Sometimes it was just necessary to accept the inevitable. They had been moving toward this moment since their first meeting. They had fought it with the tenacity of two people afraid of intimacy, but all the fighting in the world hadn't mattered. Angelle put her arms around his neck, threading her slender fingers through his curls. She let him pull her closer.

"Angel, tell me to go." Kyle's whisper was rough against her ear, sending pinpoints of feeling clear down to her toes.

"Not yet," she answered. "Don't go yet."

It was a first. She was admitting that she wanted him, that his kisses and caresses excited her. She was admitting that she cared for him. Kyle groaned. "You're supposed to tell me to go. We're supposed to fight."

"No, thank you." She pulled his mouth back to hers and began a kiss that lasted forever. This time she was the aggressor, but Kyle was not an innocent victim. His response was lightning quick, and after a second or two, no one was in charge. The kiss began as an innocent giving of affection and ended as an invitation to shared passion.

"This doesn't make any sense," Kyle whispered as he began to nibble her earlobe.

"I don't think it's supposed to," Angelle said, her voice emerging as a mere whimper. "But then, who am I to know?"

"It's not me you're responding to, Angel. You just need a man. It's not me."

She could feel his large, agile hands begin to tug her blouse loose from the waist of her skirt. When his fingers began to caress the smooth flesh of her back, she shivered in response. "Would it be easier for you if you could believe that, Kyle? And would you respond to just any woman as you're responding to me?"

He twisted the clasp of her bra and freed her breasts, his fingers moving lightly around to sweetly torture. "If you were more experienced, you'd understand these things."

"You're more experienced, and I don't think you can understand what's happening to us." And then there was no more breath for conversation, no more desire to explain herself. She lay back on the sofa, feeling the slight tremble of his fingers as he brought waves of pleasure cascading through her body.

She dug her fingers into his back as his hands caressed her breasts, and she kissed a path along his cheek. Without conscious thought, she thrust her body even closer to his.

"Do you have any idea what this is doing to me?" Kyle groaned. "I'm not a kid anymore. These little games of kiss and pet just don't do it for me. I want all of you, Angel." With a flourish he began to unbutton her blouse. "Now."

"I want you too, Kyle." Was that voice her own? She could feel the coolness of the room on her breasts as he began to slip her blouse and wispy bra over her shoulders. Suddenly aware of the lights blazing, she instinctively tried to cover herself with crossed arms, but Kyle, with great gentleness, pulled them away.

"Don't Angel. Let me look at you." She shut her eyes in embarrassment, as much for her foolish innocence as for the newness of the experience. She could feel Kyle pull away and her nerve endings tingled as his eyes swept her body.

"What do you think?" she asked in a small voice. "Will I pass inspection?"

"Inspection is only beginning." He was holding her close again, kissing her eyelids. "Open your eyes, Angel," he whispered. Soft laughter rumbled through his body when she shook her head. She felt him pull away again, and this time when he pulled her close, his shirt was unbuttoned and she could feel the soft curling hair of his chest as her breasts flattened against him.

"Oh," she said softly, and her eyes fluttered open.

"Look at us, Angel. We're so different, but the difference is perfect." He put his hand on the back of her head and forced her to look down at their bodies nestled together. Kyle was golden brown and she was pink and white. Kyle was hard and muscled; she was softly rounded. Kyle was all masculine angles, and she was all feminine curves. Her head was still reeling at the new intimacy, and she blinked in embarrassment. She shut her eyes again.

His laughter rippled through the taut muscles of his chest. "How on earth have you stayed so innocent?"

"It's been hard work," she admitted in a near whisper. She cleared her throat. "And I think it's going to be even harder in the immediate future."

His arms clasped her close, and tentatively she embraced him too. They held each other for long moments, but Angelle could feel the tension mounting around them. This was the turning point in their relationship. There was nowhere to go but back to constant bickering or forward to become lovers. All other options had been closed for them. Angelle sensed that Kyle was straining to give her time to decide.

"The truth, Angel. Can you tell me why you've never shared yourself with a man?" Kyle finally broke the silence.

She was amazed at his patience and his attempts to understand her. She doubted that many men would have cared at all. "I've been afraid," she said against his chest.

"With the right man, even the first time can be good."

She smiled, knowing that Kyle was sure he was the right man. And she had to admit it—he probably was. "That's not exactly what I meant," she explained. "I don't want a man running my life, telling me what to think, taking over my body like it was his possession." She paused. "Does that make sense?"

Kyle thought about her words. "No," he answered finally. "That's not what love is all about."

Love. A four-letter word she had never understood. Love. "Who said anything about love?" she asked, pulling away to look at him until she realized how exposed she was. Quickly she put her head back on his chest.

"God knows... I can't believe it came out of my own mouth," Kyle said. "I just assumed you were talking about it. Women always do."

"I never have."

"So you haven't been holding out for love, just for some man who promises to go his merry way when you're finished with him."

Put like that, it didn't sound quite right. Angelle furrowed her brow, trying to decide what was wrong with his statement. Finally she unwrapped her arms and with one hand, began to fish behind her for the discarded blouse. "I think it's time to call it a night," she said in her politest tone. "When our conversations get to this point, only fireworks follow."

"I can guarantee you fireworks, little lady." He brushed the blouse out of her fingers and began to trail kisses down the side of her face, along her neck, to the softness below.

"No, Kyle. Please." Angelle tried to pull away but instead found her body searching for him. "No more."

"You have no idea what you want." His mouth trailed down the hollow between her breasts and then fastened on one rigid peak.

She arched wildly toward him, moaning in immediate response. He took his time, sucking like a greedy infant, and then moved to her other breast, enjoying it the same way. Finally he hesitated for a moment, his mouth once again in the hollow between breasts. "That's desire you're feeling, Angel. The same desire a man feels when he wants to possess you."

It was the word "possess" that did it. She had been possessed all her life by men bigger and stronger than she was, who were sure they knew what was good for her. She did not ever want to be possessed that way again. With her hands on his shoulders, she tried to push him away. But Kyle was already drawing back on his own.

"I'm going to leave now. You're too confused to know if this is a good idea or not." He felt behind her for the abandoned blouse and draped it around her shoulders. She noticed that he averted his eyes as she slipped it on and buttoned enough buttons to keep it together.

"What are you thinking?" she asked softly, as he stood to leave.

"I'm wondering how I let myself get into this situation," Kyle said truthfully. He jammed his hands in his pockets and took a step away from the sofa.

It was difficult to raise her eyes to his, but she managed. This was the man, like all men, who wanted to possess her. Yet he was leaving, instinctively knowing that she wasn't ready for what he was offering. He hadn't tried to persuade, to coax, to threaten or to force. He was leaving because he knew it was what she needed. A floodgate of warmth opened inside her. Perhaps, she thought as she searched his turquoise eyes, this is what possession really is. Taking care of. Loving enough to let go. Loving.

"Kyle..."

He had turned and was already in front of the connecting door. "I'm not angry at you, Angel. It's your body, your life. Only next time..." he faced her again for a moment. "Next time, don't start something you plan to stop."

Shame swept through her, and she knew she was turning pink. "I've never been a tease. I'm sorry, Kyle."

"Thank you for dinner." He was gone, closing the door carefully behind him. She held her breath, listening for the sound of the bolt being drawn and winced when she finally heard it. Metal sliding effortlessly into metal. Kyle firmly closing her out of his life again.

But then, what could she expect? Mrs. Simpson had explored the concept of mixed messages with the adoption home-study group, and Angelle knew that tonight she had given a living demonstration of the term. Mixed messages, she had found, were when you told a person one thing and acted as if you meant something else. Angelle knew that from the beginning of her relationship with Kyle she had sent nothing but mixed messages.

Actually his messages hadn't been too clear either. The man who had fought intimacy every step of the way had been ready to carry her to bed tonight. Why? Uncomplicated desire between two consenting adults she could understand, but what was happening between them seemed larger than that. More important somehow. Confusing, upsetting, terrifying and dreadfully, dreadfully complicated.

She rose, bolted her own side of the door and carried their coffee cups into the kitchen. Immersed to her elbows in warm, sudsy water, she scrubbed each dish as if she could scrub away her own ambivalence. When she was finished, she changed into a sturdy cotton nightgown, brushed her teeth, removed her makeup and slid under the covers. She tried not to think about it, but she knew that only a few yards away, Kyle was probably in bed too.

There was something wrong with the way the evening had ended. She just wished she knew for sure what it was.

Chapter Eight

There was no peace for Kyle with Angelle living a few yards away. When he awoke in the mornings, he could smell coffee brewing, and he would lie in bed for a few lonely minutes imagining her wearing something sweetly revealing as she drifted barefoot across the floor to fix breakfast. And if it wasn't coffee he smelled, it was the faint traces of the perfume she always wore, a perfume that was rose scented and completely female.

She was like a rose, he mused one afternoon as he came home from a job early and sat on the narrow front porch watching occasional cars passing by. Sweet and delicate, needing careful tending and nurturing...and full of thorns. A surprisingly strong woman for all that fragile white skin and that incredible angel's hair.

She was a wild rose, able to survive almost anywhere, he decided.

But his final summary wasn't quite correct, and he realized it as he unlocked the front door and walked through the shotgun to the backyard to see how the dogs were. Angelle was vulnerable. Underneath the careful manners and the protests against dependency on a man was a woman who wanted to share. Not just her lovely untouched body, but her heart, her soul, her entire being.

The right man would come along, convince her that he wasn't going to swallow her whole, and she would melt into him, giving as good as she got, enriching his life immeasurably. And why did that thought give Kyle such a queer ache? He wasn't looking for that much commitment, that much merging. That much love. Love could do terrible things to people. Kyle knew that for a fact.

He unlocked the back door, stepping out onto the short porch that led into the yard. As he did, he almost stumbled over the stretched-out, lifeless body of Angelle's ridiculous cat. Gipper, the retriever, was lying beside the big Persian, his nose almost covered by long silky fur.

"Damn!" Kyle cursed. The dogs had always been perfectly calm, never attacking any other animal. Yet here lay Angelle's pride and joy, their innocent victim. "Gipper!" Kyle yelled. "What have you done?"

His answer was an ecstatic wagging of Gipper's tail, and a yawn and stretch from the miraculously recovered feline who took one calm look at Kyle, moved closer to Gipper and curled up to go back to sleep. Gipper, with what could only be called a doggie grin, put his nose down on the cat's back and shut his eyes.

"The whole world's going crazy," Kyle muttered as he pivoted and stomped back into the house.

"So how is your roommate working out?" Madame LaBois asked Angelle a week after Kyle had settled into the other side of Angelle's house.

"Roommate is not the correct term, Maw Maw. And I hardly ever see him." Angelle was examining a stain on a yellow lace formal that had been tried on one too many times. "I think this will clean nicely." She marked the price down and put it on a sale rack in the corner.

"Lover, then. So how is your lover working out?" Nonchalantly the older woman pulled a stool to the display case and began to rearrange a shelf of costume jewelry.

There was an audible gasp from the other side of the room. "The liberated old lady act does not fool me, Maw Maw."

"Just making conversation, dear."

"Just being nosy, Grandmother." The last word was drawn out into infinity.

"How is Kyle Sullivan, Angelle?"

Angelle hunched her shoulders and spread her hands apart in a 'who cares' gesture. "I have no idea. We pass on the porch; last night he borrowed two eggs. I guess he's fine."

"Such a waste, Angelle. Such a waste of human resources."

Angelle secretly agreed. She had become so finely tuned to Kyle's presence in her house that she could almost sense what he was doing at any given moment. A large portion of each evening was spent trying to think of excuses to talk to him. Once she had screwed up her courage and ventured to ask about the Korean lessons that he had mentioned they study together. But his response had been to buy her a copy of the phrase book and leave it in her mailbox. The message was clear. Kyle wanted nothing to do with her anymore.

"Kyle's not interested in me, Maw Maw. And I'm not interested in him."

"Birds don't fly and cats don't meow."

Even Miaou had deserted her, refusing to sleep inside anymore. The stupid cat preferred the company of Kyle's slobbering retrievers to Angelle's cozy house. "I wouldn't know about cats meowing. Mine is always purring, cuddled up to one of Kyle's retrievers.''

"The little things we can learn from the animal kingdom."

"Of all the grandmothers in the universe, I had to get the one who wants to see her only granddaughter lower her standards and chase blindly after a big oafish football player with a trick knee."

"That about says it all, dear." Madame LaBois pushed her stool back and rose to wink at Angelle who was standing, hands on hips, in front of the display case. "You've got the picture."

"All right. I'll go over to Kyle's tonight wearing something seductive, throw myself at his feet and tell him my grandmother sent me."

"Well, a little more finesse might be called for, but you have the general idea." Madame LaBois reached across the glass counter and tweaked Angelle's cheek. "You're not getting any younger dear."

"But I am getting smarter—" The musical tinkle of the shop bell interrupted Angelle's speech, which was just as well. Maw Maw's ideas were actually beginning to sound good to her. And she certainly didn't want her grandmother to know anything of the sort.

October in New Orleans was always a month of surprises. Usually it was warm, cooling comfortably at night, but there were occasional chilly days, and that evening as Angelle came home from a long day at the bridal shop, she was glad to have the comfort of a heavy sweater.

Perhaps it was the crispness of the air, but for the first time, as she parked her car down the street from her house and shut and locked the door, she noticed that many of the houses surrounding her had been decorated for Halloween.

No matter what the holiday, people in New Orleans gave it their all.

Without a child in the house, Halloween was only a cursory holiday for Angelle. She bought a bag of candy and tended the door, lighting a ceramic pumpkin in her window to let the neighborhood children know that they were welcome. Next year it might be different, with her own child trick-or-treating as a lovely Oriental Princess Leia or a terrifying witch. Halloween next year would be fun, if Mrs. Simpson made the right decision.

The day after Halloween was a special day in New Orleans too. All Saints' Day, only a spot on the calendar in most places, was an important event in the Crescent City. Every year on that day, since she had been old enough to remember, Angelle had made the trip across town to the beautiful Metairie Cemetery where her mother was buried. The cemetery was always crowded with relatives tending graves, placing flowers, keeping vigil. In years past, it had been a day for socializing. Wrought-iron chairs were kept by the huge family crypts and friends visited and chatted, often about the dead, just as often about the living. It was a day set aside to remember, to renew contact. Even nowadays people still mingled, although the crowds were thinner. People might not come for as long, but if they could come at all, they did.

All Saints' Day had always given Angelle the chance to talk to the mother she had never known. Her father and brothers, for once sensing her needs, had managed every year to find a way to leave her alone for a few precious minutes so that she could pour out her feelings to the woman she would have loved with all her heart. As an adult, Angelle had continued the ritual, choosing to visit the cemetery alone. She made a mental note to order a pot of chrysanthemums for her trip that year.

Coming up the front walk, she was surprised to see a dime-store cardboard cutout of a skeleton tacked to Kyle's front door. It was another sign to Angelle of what a good father he would make, and she was suffused with affection for the big man. As she stood on the porch steps examining the skeleton, his door opened slightly. "Boo!" a voice said softly.

"Boo, yourself." She stood her ground, waiting for him to join her.

"Have you eaten yet?" Kyle asked, stepping out on the porch in a lightweight T-shirt stretched across his big chest and crisp jeans that emphasized his long, muscled legs.

"You're going to freeze," she admonished. His question finally penetrated. "No, I haven't had a chance."

"Come on in—I've got homemade soup on the stove."

She was tired and cold and sad. Kyle's homemade soup could cure all three. "I'd love to."

He seemed to sense her exhaustion, and once inside, he helped her out of the sweater, refusing her offer of assistance in the kitchen. He left her to relax in the living room while he finished dinner preparations. Before she knew it, a glass of burgundy was in her hand and a hand-knit afghan was tucked around her still-chilled body.

She sat alone in his living room after he went back into the kitchen, admiring what he had done with the house. His furniture was all no-nonsense, covered in sturdy wide-wale corduroy of shades of brown and green. But there were personal touches too. One of the walls had been covered with photographs and another had a framed poster from the New Orleans Jazz Festival, which was held every spring. Angelle wanted to get up and examine the photographs; she wanted to understand Kyle better, but the wall seemed too far away. Just for a moment, she put down her wine and shut her eyes.

There was a large hand stroking her hair away from her forehead and a comfortingly warm body next to hers when, pulling herself out of unconsciousness, she realized that she had fallen asleep in Kyle's living room. "Oh," she apologized. "I'm sorry. I didn't realize I was that tired."

"It gave me a chance to put my arms around you without having to fight you."

Taking advantage of the situation, she snuggled a little closer. "Did you eat without me?"

"No, you've only been asleep a little while. Are you ready for dinner yet?"

She was ready for dinner but she wasn't ready to leave this lovely intimacy. "I don't suppose we could eat it here like this, could we?"

Kyle chuckled and, just for a moment, put his arm around her, bending over to give her a light kiss. "Come to the table, little lady. We can finish this later."

But they didn't. After a satisfying dinner of Kyle's own crabmeat-and-corn chowder and the bakery's whole-wheat rolls, Angelle leaned back in her chair and sighed. "That was terrific. Can I help you clean up?"

He shook his head, rising to give her his hand. "I have to go out in a little while. Let's relax before I do."

Relaxing seemed impossible, but she nodded, following him into the living room. Just as in her half of the shotgun, they had to walk through his bedroom to get there, and she avoided looking at the inviting king-size bed as she went by.

In the living room she settled on the sofa, but Kyle took a seat in the armchair across from her, and her disappointment was startling. They had already covered "How have you been?" and "Have you heard from Mrs. Simpson?" at dinner, and she could think of nothing more to just chat about. Kyle seemed definitely ill at ease too. Finally she ventured, "Why did you invite me tonight, Kyle?"

He reached for a box on the table, pulled out a cigar and then obviously thought better of it, slipping it back into the box before he answered. "I've missed you."

"Good. I've missed you too." They were both silent for a moment, finally breaking the silence together. "I'm sorry about Saturday."

Angelle tilted her head and blushed and Kyle reached for a cigar again, remembered, and withdrew his hand. "I really am sorry," Angelle said softly. "I didn't mean to lead you on and then pull away. I'm not like that."

"I was pushing you. You're really very vulnerable, Angel, and I knew better."

"Why did you push, Kyle?" She waited, her blue eyes fastened on his turquoise ones. "I mean, I know I'm attractive and all that, but there are women all over New Orleans who must be throwing themselves at your feet." She remembered the threat she had made to her grandmother earlier in the day. She had threatened to throw herself at his feet too, and she blushed again.

"Damned if I know, Angel."

She thought about his words and her own. Kyle had been living next door to her for a full week, and never once had there been a woman there with him. "Kyle," she asked tentatively, "are you embarrassed to bring a woman here because I'm so close by?"

"Are you trying to give me permission to bring a little playmate over for the evening, little lady?"

She winced. The thought had no appeal at all. Kyle in bed in her house with another woman. Kate Peters and Kyle in that monstrous king-size bed. She winced again. "Not at all. It's just that I created this situation when I lied to Mrs. Simpson, and I'm sorry if you're suffering for it."

"And you think that I was making love to you last week because I haven't been able to get action anywhere else?"

She blushed at the term "making love," and winced once more at his last comment. "I value myself more than that," she said with an effort.

He moved across the room and flopped down beside her. "I'm sorry, Angel. Really I am. You make me say..."

"The most outrageous things," they finished together.

"You need something I can never give you," Kyle said after a silence. "I wish it were different; I find you enormously attractive and I'd like nothing better than to carry you into that bedroom and make love to you until neither one of us can see straight. Last week, I forgot for a little while that making love to you was not a good idea."

"Why isn't it?" She had her own ideas, but she wanted to hear his version.

"You're a virgin. Whether you've figured it out or not, you've been saving yourself for some knight in shining armor who can give you the kind of commitment you deserve. Settling for less would be a wound you might not recover from."

She wondered if he was right. Had she really been holding out all these years for a very special man, a man who could fill the emptiness inside her without destroying her individuality? "I wonder..." she said out loud. "Do you suppose someone like that exists? If he doesn't, and I've really been waiting all this time, I've wasted a lot of years."

Kyle grinned, and his turquoise eyes caressed her. "If you ever decide that you've been making a mistake, I'll always be available to rectify it."

She smiled too, her dimples deepening by the moment. "Such a considerate man," she teased. "Willing to sacrifice almost anything for a friend, huh?"

He put his arm around her and turned her face to his. "You know, you really are becoming a friend. I never would have believed it was possible, but you're becoming very special to me."

Sternly she admonished her fluttering heart. An attack of the vapors right now was not appropriate at all. "And you to me," she managed to say without stuttering.

"And because you're special, I'm going to make a point of not letting anything happen between us. I don't want to spoil what we have."

She had thought the night he held her nearly naked body in his arms that there were only two possible paths for them. To become lovers or to become enemies. Friendship had seemed out of the question. She was glad that it wasn't, but she also felt like a kid who wakes up on Christmas morning to find that instead of a bike she has gotten a tricycle. Friendship wasn't enough.

Oh God, she thought, I'm in love with this man. I want all of him. I want to be his friend, his lover... his wife.

"Angel?"

She was staring at him, her huge blue eyes wide with fright and pain. "Don't you have to go somewhere?" she whispered.

"What's wrong?"

She shook her head. "Nothing." Where was the door into her apartment? Her eyes focused on the cypress panel, and she rose to look for her sweater. "Thank you for the soup. I won't keep you any longer." She slipped on the sweater, remembering just in time that the connecting door was locked on her side. She walked to the front door instead. She tried to smile as she turned to say goodbye. "I'll see you soon."

Kyle put his hands on her shoulders. "What's wrong with you. You look like you've seen a ghost."

Exactly.

"I'm just wiped out," she murmured. "I'm going to go home and crawl into bed." And pull the covers over my head and never come out again.

"Look, I wanted to ask you something. I'd like to have all the men who helped me move over for a party this weekend for Halloween. Would you mind?"

"Not at all." She turned to go.

"Would you come? As my date?"

There was no point in the world of saying no. The party would be in her backyard; she couldn't avoid it. Knowing that she'd just have to get herself under control by then, she nodded wearily. "Sure. That sounds like fun. Just let me know what I can do."

"Would you help me plan it?"

She nodded again. Her eyes drifted shut as Kyle bent to kiss her. It was a friendly kiss that was achingly tender. She wanted nothing more than to dissolve into tears when it ended. With a slight smile, she opened the door and found her way across the front porch to her own door, unlocking it and slipping quickly inside.

Her apartment was dark and cold, and she was suddenly overwhelmed with the obnoxious femininity of it all. Flowers, flowers everywhere and not a man to love. What had she let herself in for? She was twenty-six, destined to never know the comfort of a man's presence in her life simply because the man she had fallen in love with would never want her.

She had waited twenty-six years for the right man, and then like an idiot she had thrown the precious gift of her love to a man who had sworn right from the beginning that he wasn't interested. And she had almost given him everything.

Shivering, she stripped off her clothes and put on the heaviest nightgown she owned. She grabbed a quilt out of the top of her closet and threw it on the blanket that was already on the bed. Then she crawled under both of them, trembling uncontrollably.

Falling in love was like falling into a black hole in space. Everything that was important about her had completely disappeared. Everything that she had built her identity on was topsy-turvy. She was no longer Angelle the self-confident, Angelle the successful businesswoman who knew what she wanted and how to get it. She was Angelle the wreck, Angelle the stupid.

"I thought love was supposed to be fun," she whispered to Miaou who had come inside through the little swinging pet door in the kitchen. The cat prowled around the bedroom for a few moments and then disappeared again, probably to sleep with her beloved Gipper.

Well, love wasn't fun. She had never had less fun, and she had only been in love a few minutes. If it got any more intense that this, she'd be a candidate for psychiatry in an hour. Angelle sat up for a moment and punched her pillow into shape. "Damn you, Kyle Sullivan. This wasn't supposed to happen to me!"

An hour later she was still staring at the ceiling when a fierce banging almost unhinged her front door. "I'm coming," she called, pulling on her furry winter bathrobe. "Hang on."

She peeked out the front window to see Kyle rubbing his hands together. Good friend Kyle was just the person she didn't want to see, but neither did she want him to freeze to death. She opened the door reluctantly. "Forget your key?" she grumbled, trying not to notice how attractive he was in the denim and sheepskin jacket.

"May I come in?"

She gestured and he came through the door smelling of the cold, crisp air surrounding him. For a moment, she forgot to be careful. "Mmm...you smell good," she murmured.

His eyes traveled over her well-covered body. "I got you out of bed, didn't I?"

"I wasn't asleep. Have a seat."

Avoiding the love seat, she perched on a chair. "Is something wrong?"

He was grinning, his strong white teeth showing in the most engaging smile ever. "No, Angel. Something is very, very right."

For a moment she forgot to breathe. Had Kyle reached the same conclusion that she had?

But he went on. "I had to present an estimate to a woman out in Old Metairie who is building a large addition on to her house. Guess who lives next door to her?"

Angelle shrugged.

"Mrs. Simpson. She caught me as I was leaving and asked me to come talk to her for a few minutes."

Angelle was suddenly alert. "And?"

"She wanted to know how you and I were getting along now that I've moved next door. I told her the truth, that we had just been talking tonight about what good friends we had become."

"And?"

"Well, she talked to me a long time about how important raising Young Ki and Jin Ah together is, and how important it is to think of their needs and not our own."

"And?" Angelle's frustrations with his long explanation were about to become uncontrollable.

"Well, I guess I lost my temper. I told her that I understood her position, but that you and I were not children ourselves. If we said we'd be sure the children were raised together, we'd follow through." He paused for a moment and his look became sheepish. "And then I told her that we were tired of waiting, and it was time for her to make up her mind."

"And?" Angelle shouted.

"And she said yes. She's going to recommend that we adopt the kids. She said there should be no problem at all with the Korean authorities and that if we're lucky, we should each have a little Christmas present."

Angelle leaped up from her chair and threw herself at him. "I'm going to be a mother after all!" she shouted as she pummelled his big body. "And you, you big overgrown leprechaun, you're going to be a father!"

For a very long minute she forgot that their relationship was now unbearably complicated, and she let herself enjoy the feel of his strong arms around her. She lifted her head from his chest, and immediately he kissed her. It was all perfectly natural and friendly, and at first when she kissed him back, it was only a response to their good news.

But the touch of his lips reminded her of the other dimensions of their friendship, the love that had crept in while she was unaware and bound her heart to his. She tried to pull away; after all, a friendly kiss was a short kiss, but Kyle's arms tightened and his tongue began to seek hers. Suddenly the kiss wasn't friendly at all, but passion filled and hungry.

She wanted him. It would be so simple to just give up the struggle. To take what he could offer, enjoy his friendship, his body. Slowly she relaxed against him, no longer trying to pull away. Love had come for her, and he was here now. This might not be all that she wanted, but it was some of it, and it would have to be enough. She tangled her fingers in his curls, opening herself completely to his embrace, his kiss.

He accepted, slipping the robe away from her shoulders and clasping her flannel-clad body close to his. "What on earth are you wearing?" he groaned, his mouth encountering the high lace-edged collar of the gown.

"My winter nightgown," she whispered.

"I imagine that these were used for birth control in another age."

Birth control. She went cold at the thought. She was completely unprepared for him. "God, I never thought of that."

Kyle misunderstood. "If you sell these gowns at your shop, you probably shouldn't. Your brides' new husbands will despise you."

"Kyle, we can't do this." She tried to pull away.

He held her against him until she stopped trying to struggle. "Angel, nothing is going to happen. Did you think I'd already forgotten what I said a few hours ago? I'm not planning to take you to bed. I'm not trying to seduce you. Relax."

The fact that he didn't want her was the least relaxing thought she could possibly have. Something like a sob caught in her throat, and she knew she was going to cry.

"I'm sorry," he soothed, still not understanding the situation. "I was just so happy, and you're so damned tempting, little lady. But I'm under control. See? I'm carefully removing my hands; I'm breathing evenly."

"Go away," she gasped.

She could feel him stiffen beneath her, and she jumped off his lap, turning to hide her face in her hands. "You don't understand anything, you big oaf. Get out of my house!"

His hands were on her shoulders spinning her around. "What is wrong with you?"

She was crying now, big gulping sobs that shook her slender body under the voluminous gown.

"Angel, what's going on?"

"Mrs. Simpson was right," she gasped between sobs. "I can't stand you!"

He stood calmly as she continued to cry, finally offering his handkerchief as the tears began to abate. "Try again, little lady."

She shook her head, but he put two fingers beneath her chin and lifted her eyes to his. "If we're going to raise our children together, we're going to have to be honest with each other, even if it's painful. You have to tell me what's going on."

He was right. If they couldn't be open about their feelings, the crazy arrangement would never work out. But telling him that she loved him was too difficult. "Can't you guess, Kyle?" she whispered finally. "Have you no idea what you've done to me?"

He wrinkled his forehead, sending his spikey eyebrows dancing together. "What have I done?"

She started to shake her head, but stopped and shut her eyes instead. "I'm in love with you. All this friendship nonsense, all these good intentions are causing me nothing but pain. And if I keep seeing you day in and day out it's only going to get worse."

She felt his hands leave her shoulders and she sighed a shaken, devastated sigh. "I'm sorry," she said, turning so that she wouldn't have to read the sympathy in his eyes. She clutched her arms under her breasts. "Maybe I'll be able to think of a way to get over it quickly so that it won't interfere with the adoption." She tried for a desperate light touch. "Maybe I'll find some old voodoo practitioner who can give me a potion to exorcise you from my heart."

There was only silence behind her. Then, finally, Kyle's voice. "I never meant to hurt you."

"I know."

"I'm not right for you. I don't want to be in love."

"Neither did I." She was unbearably cold again. The best news of her life, the adoption of the child she would treasure forever, couldn't even touch the ice forming in her soul. "I think you should go now. When tomorrow comes, I'll be more rational. We'll talk about ways of working this complication out."

"I'm not sure that's possible now."

"Neither am I," she admitted, finally turning to face him and smile a watery smile. "But I'm sure going to try. I won't lose my daughter over a big Irish oaf."

He tried to smile back at her, but it didn't reach his eyes. Gratefully Angelle saw that there was no pity there either. "I'll see you tomorrow, then," he said.

"Yes, tomorrow."

He turned and walked to the front door. "You could be mistaken. We've wanted each other from the first day we met. You could just be admitting to desire for the first time, Angel."

"That would be very easy to find out if I wanted to put it to the test, wouldn't it?" she said. "But then sleeping with you could make it much worse for me if it wasn't just . . . desire."

"Yes, it could make it much, much worse."

"That's too bad, isn't it," she whispered. "Because I do want to sleep with you very, very much."

If he was shocked by her bluntness, he didn't let on. "For what it's worth, I want you too. More than I've ever wanted a woman before."

"It's worth something. Just not enough."

He opened the door and she could feel the gust of chilling air blow right through her. "Tomorrow," he said, and closed the door behind him.

Tomorrow they would sit down and casually solve the worst crisis of her existence. Tomorrow the sky might turn green too. She found her way back under the covers and cried herself to sleep.

Chapter Nine

It took a frantic phone call from Madame LaBois to get Angelle out of bed the next morning. Once she had finally fallen asleep, she had slipped into a near-coma state so deep that the phone only sounded like an annoying mosquito. She was an hour late, and although there was sufficient help at the shop to cover her absence, Madame LaBois was furious.

"I'm sorry, Maw Maw. I'll be there as soon as I dress." Angelle stretched, rumpling her hair with one hand as she listened to her grandmother's righteous complaints. "Yes, I know you were worried. I apologize." Finally she held the receiver away from her ear until there was no longer sound from the other end. "I'll see you in a few minutes," she said and quickly hung up.

"Fall in love," she muttered as she searched groggily for something to wear, "and your life begins to disintegrate immediately. Fall in love and you become a basket case."

There was a sharp rapping at her front door, and combing her fingers through her tangled hair, she stumbled to open it. Too bleary-eyed to even follow normal security procedures, she didn't even peek out the window. Opening the door, she was surprised to see Kyle standing there. His presence shook her out of her dazed lethargy, and she had a distinct vision of what she must look like.

"Go away," she said simply as she tried to shut the door.

Kyle's foot lodged firmly in the doorway. "No way, little lady."

It was still cold outside, and the rush of air through the open door threatened to turn her white skin blue. "Suit yourself," she said, shivering. "But you're not invited to come in, and I'm going to go get dressed."

"You'd leave me here to freeze?"

"That would certainly solve my problems."

"As nasty in love as you were out of it."

She gasped at his bad taste and whirled to confront him, surprised by the friendly humor on his face. "Oh, all right," she said with a shrug. "Come on in." She walked back through the house.

"I want to talk to you."

"Talk, then. I'm going to get dressed." She was completely awake now and already slipping back under the spell of last night. She wanted nothing more than to sit next to him on the love seat and feel his warmth enveloping her. His arms would be hard and sure as they came around her and his mouth... She shook herself. That kind of behavior was out of the question completely.

He followed her into the little sitting room next to her bedroom, and she put her hands up in defense as he began to follow her into her bedroom. "Whoa, there. I'm going to get dressed and you're definitely not invited to watch."

"It would make my morning."

"Make it some other way."

There was no door between the two rooms, a situation she had planned to remedy when Jin Ah arrived. Angelle grabbed a dress from her closet and scooted into the corner away from the open doorway to dress. Her fingers were fumbling in her haste to cover herself, and halfway up the back of the aqua wool dress, the zipper rebelled and decided to retire. The dress was too tight to slip back off. "Terrific!" she yelled. "My zipper's stuck and it's your fault."

A rumble of laughter rolled in from the sitting room. Kyle appeared in the doorway. "If it's my fault, then I should have to fix it. After all, what are neighbors for?"

"Not for falling in love with, that's for darned sure," she muttered under her breath. "Make yourself useful, then." She turned, exposing a broad expanse of creamy skin to his view. There wasn't even a bra or a slip to mar the sight.

"My God, Angel. Don't you usually wear something under your dresses?" His voice sounded shaken, and she felt a smile trying to break out of the fog of depression she had slipped into the night before.

"Not when I'm in a hurry. Besides," she said matter of factly, "you should know that with my figure, all those foundations only flatter a faltering ego."

He chuckled, allowing his fingers to brush her spine repeatedly as he worked with the zipper. "You are absolutely perfect, little lady. There's not a thing about you that I'd want to change. Dolly Parton, eat your heart out."

She giggled, and the sound amazed her. She could still smile, she could still laugh, even with Kyle's fingers torturing the innocent skin of her backbone. Love may have set her back a little, but it hadn't killed her. "Why did you come?" she asked, changing the subject.

"I wanted to talk about last night."

"Well, I'm a captive audience. Go ahead."

"I don't know what to say."

"Me either."

She felt the zipper move down the track toward her waist. "Oh, did you fix it?"

"Not yet." His hands were still stroking her back as he worked on the feisty strip of plastic teeth.

"My grandmother is going to slice me into pieces. I'm already an hour late for work."

As if to strengthen her point, the telephone rang. Angelle could just reach it by leaning over and Kyle bent with her, continuing his exploration of her smooth skin.

"Hello? Yes, I'm still here. My zipper is stuck." Angelle held the telephone away from her ear in exasperation. When the flood of abuse had stopped, she said calmly. "You'll be pleased to know that the man of your dreams is here right now trying to fix it for me, and taking his sweet time about it too."

There was dead silence on the other end for a moment and then the conciliatory voice of her grandmother came over the line.

Angelle listened, hoping that Kyle couldn't hear the older woman's words. "Yes, Maw Maw. I'm still coming in. No, I don't want the day off. I'm glad you think you understand the situation." She listened for a moment and then almost hissed into the phone, "No, I didn't serve him breakfast in bed." She hung up the phone with a bang.

"Whew! That's quite an old lady!"

Angelle slapped her hands on her hips. "Your biggest fan."

"And how does she know about me?"

"She reads my mind. Aren't you finished yet?"

"Actually I've been finished for a long time. It was just too enjoyable to admit it." She could feel the zipper slide to its apex. "Since you don't have to rush in to work, let's go sit and talk."

"No, I still have to get in as quickly as possible or Maw Maw will be sure you and I are indulging in a little early morning delight, and she'll be impossible to live with."

"She didn't sound too protective to me."

"Not in the way you mean." Angelle had avoided turning to face him, but his big hands on her shoulders did it for her.

"Let me make some coffee and toast for you, Angel. We can talk over a quick breakfast."

She wanted to trace his funny eyebrows and run her fingers through his unruly curls. And she wanted to kiss the tender smile off his wide, hard mouth. "All right," she said in defeat.

"Better yet, you could serve me breakfast in bed like your grandmother suggested."

"Kyle, I can't take that kind of teasing anymore." She took a deep breath. "What if I take you up on that offer? Do you want a woman in your bed who loves you? It would complicate your life immeasurably. And mine too."

His face settled into serious lines. "I can't tell you how much I'll miss teasing you, Angel. Don't cut me out of your life just because you have the mistaken idea that you're in love with me. You've been a breath of fresh air, and I don't want to lose you."

His words were a plea, and they astonished her. "What can I say to that?" she whispered. "You know I don't want to lose you either. I'm in love with you, for God's sake."

"You think you're in love with me. I thought about this last night, and I want to tell you what I think is happening." With an arm draped casually over her shoulder he pushed her into the kitchen. "Sit down, I'll make you some coffee and then we'll talk."

She told him where to find everything and then watched him move competently around her kitchen. He was all man, but he could manage kitchen chores like the most efficient homemaker. Finally he was sitting at the small kitchen table, grimacing at her hyacinth-covered tablecloth. "More flowers."

"Yes," she sympathized. "Nauseating, aren't they."

His mouth turned up in a half grin. "Angel, before I tell you what my analysis of this situation is, I want to tell you that I think you're one terrific lady."

Her etiquette instructor in high school would have been charmed with that evaluation. Angelle wasn't. "Thank you," she said quietly. "Now let's have it."

"Well," he said, fumbling around for a place to start, "I think that you're mistaking desire fused with friendship for love. We've wanted each other from the first time we met. And due to a series of unavoidable events, we've been thrown together in intimate circumstances time and time again. We've been forced to probe each other's psyche, forced to live together. We've had to adapt or not adopt."

Angelle sipped her coffee and examined her nails, refusing to look in his direction. "And?"

"Well, don't you see? All this forced togetherness has you confused. You've kind of gotten used to having me around, depending on me to understand your feelings about the adoption. And I've gotten used to having you around to tease, to touch when you'd let me. We've just fallen into the habit of needing each other. Put that on top of desire and it gets confusing. But it's not love."

His logic was ridiculous, but hidden somewhere in the careful explanation was a shining ray of hope. He was admitting that he had feelings for her too, the same feelings she had for him, only he couldn't yet define them as the big four-letter word.

"Well, what do you think?" he asked hopefully. "Aren't I right?"

"You say the most outrageous things, Kyle Sullivan." She lifted her eyes to his. "Now define love for me. If it isn't desire mixed with need, and a strong feeling of comfort and joy in each other's presence, then what is it? I'm sure I have no idea."

As she watched, the color seemed to drain out of his face, starting at the top of his forehead. "I'm not in love," he choked. "My God, I didn't even like you at first."

She had thought that her dimples would never be used again, but she flashed them at him. "I didn't like you either, remember? I thought you were the most disgusting man I'd ever encountered."

"I am not in love. I will not be in love!"

"Have it your way," she soothed him. "After all, you have a right to your own feelings, as Mrs. Simpson would say."

"What are you trying to do to me, Angel?"

Her ears perked up at his tone. What was she trying to do to him? This macho jock had pushed his way into her life, turned it upside down, and now he wanted to know what she was doing? "Not one blasted thing, you inflated egotist. I don't even want to give you enough rope to hang yourself. Live your life exactly the way you want. I don't care."

"If you don't care, then you're not in love with me!"

She stood up and pushed the table toward him as she did. "You're probably right. I'm probably not in love with you. Who could love an Irish football-playing oaf anyway? I'm glad you've made me realize it so quickly." She was shouting. "Now we can go back to being good friends!"

He jumped up and shouted back. "Good friends! Now you've got it. We'll continue to be the best of friends. No more talk of love, Angel little lady Reed!"

"The word won't escape my lips again until I meet a man worthy of it."

"Good!"

She took a calming deep breath and then smiled her sweetest smile. "Now if you don't mind, I'm going to go to

the bathroom and finish getting dressed for work. So nice
to have had this time with you." She turned at the bathroom door. "Have a nice day, friend."

"You too, friend." They stared at each other for a minute. "Will you still come to the party this weekend?" he
asked.

"What are friends for?"

"I'll talk to you about the arrangements later." She
watched him retreat. At the door, without turning his head,
he muttered, "A man could choke on the fumes from all
these flowers."

"A man could choke on his own feelings too," she said
too softly for him to hear. "Especially if he doesn't admit
that he has them." She stood thinking about her own words
for long minutes before she turned and went into the bathroom.

Kyle's Halloween party grew like an overweight matron
released from a corset. From a simple cookout for a few
friends it expanded to a full-fledged New Orleans extrava-
ganza. Kyle kept thinking of friends he should invite, and
politely, in her friendliest manner, Angelle encouraged him.
Throwing parties was not her favorite endeavor—it was too
much like her job—but planning a party did give her a
chance to interact with Kyle in a casual way. And it kept her
busy.

Angelle baked a ham and Kyle smoked a turkey. A local
deli was contacted to do the rest. In a fit of holiday fever,
Kyle bought miles of black and orange crepe paper to decorate Angelle's backyard like a sophisticated two-year-old's
nightmare. Kyle kept his costume a secret, and Angelle, who
had a surplus of appropriate wear, decided to go as an angel.

Saturday dawned warm and sunny, and Angelle worked
side by side with Kyle to set up rented tables under the trees
in her yard. She was acutely aware of him, vibrating inter-

nally every time he got within three feet. It was almost as if someone had installed a Kyle alarm inside of her. Still, she refused to let him see the effect he induced. She was charming, witty and only a friend, no matter what.

Kyle, for his part, was friendly too, but he seemed to take great pains to avoid touching her, stepping out of her way when he could, taking things out of her hands with absolutely no brushing of fingers. When they talked, he stayed a polite distance away, meeting her eyes when he had to, smiling if it was really called for.

"Kyle," she said finally, when once again he had stepped neatly around her, "you don't have to avoid me quite so strenuously. I'm just fine. I won't fall screaming at your feet if you accidentally touch me."

His expression could only be classified as irritated. "I didn't think that you would."

"Well, you're giving a good imitation of a man who thinks something is terribly wrong." She was throwing tablecloths on the tables, weighting them down with platters that would eventually be filled with food.

"I just don't want to give you any ideas."

"I see. You're afraid I might forget myself and attack you." She purposely dimpled. "Not to worry."

"That is not what I meant!" he barked at her.

"Touchy, aren't we?"

"You are asking for trouble, little lady."

It was the first time in the three days since their confrontation about the meaning of love that he had used his pet name for her. This time her dimples were spontaneous. "I have never had to look any further than the nose on your face if I wanted trouble," she said, her tone dripping honey.

"You think you've had trouble? I'll give you trouble, Angel. Come here." Kyle threw the bag of decorations he was carrying on the nearest table and began to stalk her.

Standing her ground didn't seem like a very good idea, and Angelle began to back away slowly. "Whatever you have in mind is not a good idea," she pointed out. "I can guarantee it."

"Come here, Angel." He crooked his finger at her as he continued to move closer, shoulders hunched as if he were ready to spring.

"I'll pass on this, if you don't mind. I think I ought to check and make sure the ham is warmed through."

"Come here, Angel." Without warning he lunged and grabbed the lapels of the candy-striped blazer she wore. "Now you'll see why I've been avoiding you."

"You were afraid of wrinkling my blazer?" she asked innocently before his mouth ground down on hers.

Provoking him backfired. The rush of victory she felt at his response to her teasing was instantly quelled by the strongest emotion she had ever felt in her life. Her body exploded, leaving her drained of will, thought erased. All she could do was respond. From the distance she heard a whimper, and she knew it had come from her own throat.

Kyle lifted her against him, letting her feel his own arousal and the sensation left her shaking with need. His tongue mimicked what they both wanted, plunging into her mouth with such fierce desire that she could only acquiesce, could only allow it to happen. Holding on tightly, she trembled against him when he finally moved his mouth from hers. "So, Angel, is this what you were after?"

"I wasn't after anything," she said tearfully. "What are you trying to do to me?"

He dropped her unceremoniously on her feet, waiting a scant second to be sure she could stand before he stepped back. "It's what I'm not trying to do to you that's the problem. I may not love you, but I sure as hell want you. And if you keep teasing me, you're going to find yourself compromised. Completely."

Watching as he grabbed the decorations and stalked off to the other side of the yard to begin stringing crepe paper streamers, she was absolutely sure that he meant what he'd said.

She realized as she retreated to the kitchen to begin slicing the ham that they had switched roles. At first Kyle had been the one who had been disappointed when she had asked him to stop teasing her. Now he was threatening her for doing the same to him. She really hadn't meant to provoke him, not to the point she had anyway. She had only wanted to break through the polite fortress he was building against her. The entire situation was hopeless. They would never fine-tune it. No matter what, friendship with Kyle was doomed to failure. All because she had allowed herself to fall in love and then to tell him about it.

The ham was a terrific vehicle for her pent-up frustrations, and when she was finished, the ten-pound piece of pork had been mutilated into tiny bits and pieces. When she peeked outside, Kyle's streamers had transformed her backyard into a tacky Halloween display. He was gone, probably to the delicatessen to pick up the salads he had ordered. Angelle took the opportunity to shower and change into the white cotton dress that she had last worn to the symphony the night of her abortive date with Dennis.

She had purchased a wide silver headband, and she tied it around her forehead like an extravagant hippy. It served as her halo, and for wings she had tied yards of silver lamé into a giant bow and pinned it discreetly to the back of her dress. "Purity personified," she said, gazing in the mirror. Her hair was a white cloud falling to her shoulders, and her skin was pale with rose-kissed cheeks. She hadn't even darkened her eyelashes or eyebrows, and she looked like an innocent teenager, if such a phenomenon existed.

"I should have gone as a vamp," she decided as her own vigilantly chaste appearance overwhelmed her. Being a amp would have meant a new dress, a new hairstyle, new makeup. "But at least everyone would have known I was in costume!"

She wondered if there was time to make the change. Setting down with the yellow pages, she called the nearest costume shop. Since New Orleanians invariably dressed in costumes for Mardi Gras and any other event they could justify, outrageous outfits of every kind were readily available for rent.

Half an hour later she arrived back at the house, box in ow. Anything resembling a vamp costume had already been ented to Halloween's female Draculas, but Angelle had ound something that she thought might do instead. She hook the skimpy costume out, said a short prayer of thanks hat it was a warm day and slipped it on. Long black stockings accentuated her slender legs all the way up to the top of er thighs where the rest of the costume began. She fasened the stockings with black lace garters and then traightened the short black pleated skirt. The white satin louse was sleeveless and had no back, though it was demure enough in front, with pleats and a little black bow tie.

Piling her hair on top of her head, she fastened the ruffled black cap. "At your service, monsieur," she cooed into he mirror as she applied more makeup than she usually wore in a week. Finished, she admired her image. A little French maid beamed back at her. And there was nothing ngelic about her.

She was dumping ham onto platters when Kyle's guests egan to arrive. He was greeting them as they came in hrough the house and he had not seen Angelle since their kiss earlier in the day. Guests swarmed through the backard, introducing themselves and getting into the swing of hings immediately by heading right for the keg of beer on he small patio.

Although she was officially his date, Angelle didn't eve
see Kyle for the first half hour. After mingling and enjoy
ing the casual flirting of several men, she climbed the porc
steps to replenish a platter of ham and to bring out mor
hard rolls. There on the steps, with fire in his eyes, stoo
Kyle.

He was dressed as a riverboat gambler, complete wit
sleazy brocade vest and shiny bowler hat with an ace on th
hat band and in the garter on his sleeve. Even in the crow
of crazier and more exotic costumes, he stood out, tall an
ruggedly handsome. "Just what do you call that get-up?"
he asked in a voice that was not casual at all.

"I'm a French maid. Don't you like it?" Wickedly sh
pivoted, making sure that he got the total picture. See if h
called her little lady now.

"I'll handle the party while you change."

"*Mais non, monsieur.*" Her French failed. "I'm happ
just the way I am."

"Every man here is getting ideas about you." He took he
arm and pulled her toward her back door. "Go change."

Her anger flared. At the party were two harem girls, on
Playboy bunny, and one woman who might as well hav
come as Lady Godiva. No one was offended. The stan
dards of good taste had all been reached but not exceeded

"Good friends don't tell each other how to dress. Yo
have no rights where I'm concerned." She pulled her arm
from his. "Excuse me so I can see to your guests."

She left him standing on the porch with a look on his fac
that could have boiled water. Inside the kitchen, her hand
shook from the confrontation. She had not worn the cost
ume to make him angry. It had been an attempt to show hin
that she too had a playful, sexy side. She was not a prude
only a virgin.

She filled the platter and considered his request. Re
quest? Hardly that. It had been an order, and orders, es

ecially from a man, had no appeal for Angelle. With her head erect she carried the platter back outside. She would remain a little French maid.

Kyle studiously ignored her for the next hour, not even looking in her direction. But finally he gravitated toward her, pulling her arm through his in a proprietary gesture after one smitten young man, dressed as a Regency dandy, had begun to follow her around a bit too closely. Some of Kyle's friends were amateur musicians, and they had set up an impromptu jam session on the patio. Kyle pulled her over to stand beside him as he opened his trumpet case and proceeded to join them.

Several of the couples from their adoption home study were there, and eventually, her eyes still on Kyle, Angelle drifted toward them to find out how their plans were proceeding. One of the couples was expecting to have a baby placed in their home at any time, and the other had decided to adopt a toddler with multiple handicaps. Both were equally thrilled with their approaching placements. Angelle shared her news and received her share of hugs.

It was very late when the party began to wind down. Angelle was gossiping with Lisa and Roy when Kyle flopped down beside her to sit for the first time during the long evening. By the time Lisa and Roy made their excuses and said goodbye, there was no one else left.

"You throw quite a party," she said as casually as she could manage. The long night had gone by with almost no words exchanged between them.

"I really appreciated your help," he said in an obvious attempt at reconciliation. "My friends are all raving about you."

"About me or the costume?"

He ignored her comment. "Where did you learn to put everyone at their ease like that?"

"Did I put you at ease too? I'm glad. You were pretty wrought up before the party began." She rose to begin clearing away the few plates that were left.

"Don't do that. Come with me." He took the plates from her hands and pulled her beside him.

Acquiescent, she allowed him to propel her into the house. They passed through his kitchen, and she fully expected to keep going into the living room, but instead he stopped beside the king-size bed that took up most of his bedroom. "This is where I've pictured you all day." He sat heavily, pulling her to stand between his legs. "We can't go on the way we have been."

She rested her hands on his bronzed curls, wishing with all her heart that he could have said something different, but she let him pull her closer and wrap his arms around her hips anyway. "What are you saying?" she asked huskily.

"I'm saying that I can't live here like this. God, Angel, I had no idea in the world that you could do this to me when I agreed to this crazy arrangement. At the time all I wanted was to adopt one parentless Korean boy. But I didn't know what I was getting myself into."

She stroked his head, her body buzzing brightly with the feel of it on her stomach. "How do you suppose we should take care of the problem, Kyle?"

"There are only two choices. Either we sleep together, get it out of our systems, or I'm going to have to move out."

You could love me, marry me, she thought. That would solve the problem too. But saying that out loud would be ridiculous. She couldn't make Kyle love her. "We may lose the children if you move away."

"I saw a house down the street that looks like it might be appropriate for Young Ki and me. I think I can convince Mrs. Simpson that I just needed more room. I'll still be willing to make sure the children see each other frequently."

"I come with that package, remember? You'll have to see me too."

Slowly he unwrapped his arms. "It sounds like you want me to go."

"It would be best," she said woodenly.

"I could persuade you to let me love you tonight, and we both know it."

"What a funny choice of words..."

"Angelle, I care about you more than I've ever cared about a woman. I want you so much I feel like a teenager again. I trust you, I like you, but that's all I can say. If I make love to you, it will have to be enough."

With his hands on her waist, he lay back on the bed, bringing her with him. Sometime during the evening he had taken off his vest and jacket, and she had unpinned her hat and taken her hair down. They were no longer characters in a Halloween fantasy, they were a man and a woman, and they both ached for the fulfillment of those roles.

"Take me to heaven, Angel. Let me find it in you." With his arms around her he pinned her beneath him, beginning a ravaging assault on her senses that was like nothing she had ever experienced. When he had kissed her before, she had thought that he was unrestrained, but now she realized just how careful he had been. He was not careful now. He wanted her; he was determined to get what he wanted.

There was no time to make a decision. Every cell of her body was invaded with treacherous languor. All she could do was sigh and make soft animal noises as he ravished her with his tongue and teeth and with his strong agile hands. If she could have gathered her resources to try to resist him, it would have been futile. But there were no resources to gather anyway. If she had been given a week to decide what to do, her answer would have been the same. Her "parent," in the form of her Grandmother, had given her permission, and her "child" wanted him desperately. Only the "adult" part of her was strangely silent.

She felt the cool evening air on her legs and she knew that her stockings were off, but she didn't care. Kyle unsnapped the band of the little pleated skirt and sought her slender waistline, covering her soft skin with his warm hand. His thumb traced restless patterns on the smoothness of her abdomen, and the new intimacy was unbearably pleasurable. She thought briefly of the years she had waited to yield her body. Waited for love. Well, she had found love. Surely now was the right time.

"Let me slip this off," he whispered in her ear. "Let me love you."

It was funny that he kept using that word. The man who didn't want love, kept asking to love her. The "adult" part of her mind caught the irony and resounded with it. Making love...love. Loving someone...being loved. Having love...giving love.

"No."

Instantly his hand stilled, coming to rest on her abdomen.

"No." She pushed him away easily, sitting up to shake her hair around her shoulders. "I won't settle for part of you. I know you can't give more, but I can't take less."

On shaking legs she stood and gathered her stockings and shoes, self-consciously straightening her skirt. "I'm not a little tease, and I'm not a sexy little French maid. I'm just me, and I say no. This isn't right for me, although I wish with all my heart that it was."

"Angel." Kyle was sitting up now, running his hand through his curls. "What will you have to keep you warm in the long nights ahead? Your refusal to become a woman?"

"No. I'll have my integrity." She felt a tear run down her cheek. "And maybe someday I'll find a man who wants me because of that."

"Angel..."

She held up her hand. "No more. I'm not angry at you. We've both let this happen. We've both pushed until there was no place else to go, nothing left to do." She turned to face him. "I'd like you to move as soon as possible. Right now I'm too upset to know if we should go through with this adoption. When we've both calmed down we'll have to level with Mrs. Simpson and make our decision with her help."

With control that she didn't feel, Angelle managed to walk through the kitchen and out onto the back porch. She let herself in through her own kitchen door.

Methodically she wrapped and put away the remaining leftover ham and cleaned up the dishes. Anyone observing her would have thought that having a clean kitchen mattered. Only Angelle knew that at that moment; nothing mattered at all.

Chapter Ten

Monday night was trick or treat night, and Angelle dutifully handed out candy to the tiny ghosts and goblins that came to her front door. Kyle's side of the house was dark and forebidding. Cardboard skeleton and other decorations notwithstanding, he had chosen to spend his evening somewhere else.

Watching the children parade by was one of the most difficult things Angelle had ever had to do. Each little costumed body spoke to her of her own loss. No matter how she ached to become a mother, she had firmly put aside the fantasy of taking her own daughter trick-or-treating the next year. When she and Kyle finally sat down with Mrs. Simpson, she knew what the verdict would be. There were too many emotional complications to make their situation a good one for Young Ki and Jin Ah.

A Korean family who evidently lived on Calhoun came by with three little girls dressed in authentic Korean costume. It was the final knife twisting in Angelle's heart to see the three, stair-step little beauties as they held out their plastic Halloween pumpkins to accept the handfuls of candy she gave them. She knew it wasn't true, but at that moment, she felt that she had lost everything important in her life, and the devastation she experienced was frightening.

At nine o'clock she turned off her front porch light. There had been no lisping "trick or treats" at her door for almost an hour. It was too early to go to bed, too late to start a project. There was nothing to read; she disliked television. With the fatalism born of other nights just like it, she undressed and slid under the covers. Forcing her eyes closed, she began a long night of sleeplessness early.

Kyle woke up Tuesday morning with a hangover. He had drifted from Halloween party to Halloween party the night before, imbibing more than he should have at each one. Not one of the parties had been fun. Several of his friends had asked him where his beautiful blond French maid was, and several more had asked him when the impending wedding was going to take place. Astonished that they could misread the situation so totally, he had laughed off the queries, not having the energy to explain himself.

In the spirit of the holiday, a ghost from Kyle's past had come back to haunt him at the last party he attended. His ex-wife, Dale, was visiting New Orleans, and along with the Dallas Cowboy she had recently become engaged to, she had been invited to the party. It had been an unpleasant shock to see her fused to the arm of the proud, balding quarterback.

Dale looked much the same, although her hair was now a frosted brown and she was noticeably older. They had mumbled a few polite words and avoided each other for the rest of the night, but he had been able to watch her across the room, and he was surprised that he had ever thought that she and Angelle were anything alike.

Both women were small and deceptively fragile, and they both looked as if they needed to be taken care of. But neither did. Dale would always manage. She would find a man to provide her with the excitement she craved, and when she tired of him, or he of her, she would find another. Expediency was Dale's middle name.

Kyle knew that Angelle would manage too. She had exhibited a strength of character that he had not seen up close for years, and that strength would move her through the disappointments of her life. He had poured another drink and refused to remember how many drinks had come before, but the liquor had only increased the emptiness he felt. Surrounded by his friends, he had never felt more alone.

On Tuesday morning, Kyle lay in bed, forcing his eyes to focus and his mind to stop whirring. It was All Saints' Day and he had given his crews the day off. All Saints' Day wasn't even a public-school holiday anymore, but Kyle was old New Orleans, and the day mattered to him.

He fixed a quick breakfast, trying not to listen to the faint sounds from next door. When he heard Angelle's front door slam and the sound of a car pulling away from the curb, he unlocked the back door and went outside to toss a tennis ball to the two retrievers. Angelle's big Persian was nowhere in sight—keeping a low profile, he decided, just like her owner.

Instead of his customary casual clothing, Kyle pulled on a dark green sports coat and threaded a tie under the collar of a dress shirt. A short trip to the florist and two bronze chrysanthemum plants later, he was on his way to the Metarie Cemetary to visit the crypt that held the bodies of his parents.

Mark Twain had commented in his reminiscences, *Life on the Mississippi*, that "there is no architecture in New Orleans except in the cemeteries." Kyle wasn't sure that he agreed, but certainly he was impressed, as always, by the ornate city of the dead. The cemetery was not a bleak place.

Landscaped with cedar, magnolia, live oak and sable palm, it was a park covered with monuments to the departed, and wandering through it was the same as taking a sojourn into the area's colorful history.

There were granite tombs marked by statues of angels and of Confederate soldiers. There was a tomb guarded by a faithful marble dog who was mysteriously decorated with a collar of flowers every All Saints' Day, and there were the tombs of famous and infamous characters who had given so much to Louisiana. Today, Kyle ignored them all, walking with a heavy sense of purpose to the middle of the cemetary where the vault that had been his family's since the turn of the century was placed.

He passed models of ornate Greek temples, adaptations of Athenian towers and a fifteen-ton Celtic cross before he came to the red polished granite tomb, simple in design, where his parents rested. In years past he had dutifully come, placed his pots in the marble urns, said a prayer or two and left quickly. Today he needed to do more.

There was no wrought-iron bench at this tomb, and he sat on the ground beside it, wondering, at first, why he was still there. His parents had died while he was a college student, first his mother, then his father following closely behind. Kyle had accepted their deaths and gone on with his life, maintaining family ties with an older brother who lived in California, and with numerous cousins who still lived in Louisiana.

Being there on that day, really being there, seemed vital somehow. He didn't often think of his childhood or of the people who had given him life, but he let his mind drift back, wondering what he would find. Relaxing for the first time in days, he relished the sun shining brightly on his shoulders, and he took off his jacket, tossing it on the ground beside him.

"Kyle?"

He was surprised at the voice, and he raised his eyes to see Angelle, dressed in white, standing on the road in front of his family's tomb. She was a vision, and he blinked, wondering when he had gotten superstitious. "Angel."

"I...I didn't expect to find you here," she said in a small voice.

"Where are you going?"

"I've already been...to my mother's tomb."

He noticed a tear streak down her cheek and a smudge of loose dirt on the white dress. She looked as if she needed comfort, and he knew he was the last person to give it to her. It made no sense in the world, but he lifted his hand and she came to join him as he spread his coat for her to sit on.

"Have you never said goodbye?" he asked softly, taking out his handkerchief to wipe her cheek.

"I never even said hello. My mother died a year after I was born. I never knew her."

The most feminine woman he had ever known, raised by men. It was another example of her strength of character. "She would have loved you," he said.

"Yes, I know. That didn't always help, though."

"I'm sure."

They sat in silence. "What about your family, Kyle?" she asked, a polite prelude to her departure.

He never talked about his parents, not to anyone. But she had asked, and for some reason, he wanted to share. "Both my parents have been dead for over a decade."

"I'm sorry," she said, putting her hand on his for a moment. "At least you had them for a while."

He thought about her words. "They were good people. The most extraordinary thing about them was how very much they were in love with each other. My father died of a broken heart after my mother was killed in a car accident. He couldn't live without her."

He had never said those words to anyone. Officially, of course, his father had died of something else. But everyone who knew Carl and Laura Sullivan knew differently. "He couldn't live without her," Kyle said, biting off the words. "That's what love does to people."

He looked up to see the shocked expression on Angelle's face. "Would you have wished it was any different for them?" she asked hesitantly. "They had each other. That was more than most people are given in a normal lifetime."

"My father had two sons who needed him, and a fulfilling career. He chose not to go on. That's what love does to people."

"You're so wrong," Angelle said with soft conviction. "That's what loss does to people. Loneliness kills too, Kyle. Only giving love and letting it be given to you makes people strong."

"My father was weak, and he had been much loved."

"Your father couldn't accept any love except your mother's, and that's sad, but it doesn't have to be that way."

She stood to leave as if she sensed that he should be alone again. "I'm sorry," she apologized. "You don't need an argument right now, do you?" Spontaneously she bent and kissed the top of his head as if, even in her own pain, she wanted to bestow comfort. "Take care, Kyle."

In a moment she was walking down the road, a drifting vision of white against the ornate marble tombs. He watched her go until there was nothing left to watch. And he wondered if it always hurt this much to lose... a friend.

Angelle went to the bridal shop and relieved her grandmother so that Madame LaBois could pay her own visits to the cemetery. The day dragged, as all days had lately, and when the time came to lock up the shop, she did it competently but with little enthusiasm. Now the evening would drag, and then the night.

Her brother Michael had invited her to come to his house for a traditional family get-together. It would be a chance for everyone to meet and talk over old times since their busy schedules didn't permit them getting together at the cemetary. For the first year ever, Angelle refused the invitation, claiming that she wasn't feeling well and needed an evening's rest. She was sure Michael wasn't fooled, since Madame LaBois was his grandmother too and never had been able to keep information to herself. But Angelle couldn't summon up the energy to care what Michael or Charles or John thought. She wanted to be alone.

There were lights on in Kyle's side of the house, and just for a moment Angelle stood on the short walk leading from the street to her house, remembering the night that he had invited her in for chowder. That had been the night of her revelation about her feelings for him. It had been the beginning of the end. She shuddered and walked quickly up onto the porch.

Kyle's door opened and she heard his voice behind her. "Angelle?"

She stood key in hand, staring at her doorknob.

"Have you had dinner yet?"

She shook her head, blond hair floating around her face.

"Please eat with me."

She shook her head again.

Then she felt the warmth of his body beside her and the strength of his arm encircling her slender shoulders. "Please?" he said, his breath tickling her cheek.

"Oh, Kyle," she said a half sob in her throat, "I just can't."

"We have to talk. I have to talk. Come on, Angel. This has to happen. Let it happen."

She let him guide her into his living room and over to the comfortable corduroy sofa. He sat next to her with his arm still around her shoulders. "I have to know," he said in a voice that was strangely different from his usual, "I have to know if you're as miserable as I am."

"How miserable are you?" she asked in a small voice.

"Miserable enough to dig a hole and crawl into it."

She nodded.

"Miserable enough to shovel dirt over my head and pack it down."

She nodded.

"Miserable enough to want to stay there forever."

She nodded again.

"That's pretty miserable, don't you think?"

"Yes." She glanced at him and then looked quickly away.

"So what are we going to do about it?"

She let her eyes search the room. There was no sign of boxes being packed. "I thought the solution was for you to move away," she said with a catch in her voice.

"Well, I don't feel any better when I'm away from here, and I've been away as much in the last couple of days as I possibly could be."

"What do you suggest we do, then?"

"I made one suggestion and you turned it down."

She knew he was referring to her refusal to go to bed with him. "And I would have to turn you down again. That's no answer—at least it isn't for me." She tried to pull away, but he tightened his arm around her.

"Angel, I think I've come up with another possible solution."

"If you have," she said sadly, "it will take divine intervention to make it work. This situation seems to be beyond the help of mortal man."

"Well, actually, an angel showed me the way." He turned her to face him, their bodies only inches apart. His mouth dropped toward hers. "It's so very simple, but then the best plans always are." He kissed her before she could move away, letting his tongue prod her mouth with gentle insistence. "Open for me, Angel. Give me the strength I need to say this."

She sighed, unable to withhold herself from him. His tongue touched hers and his arms tightened. She could feel his strength everywhere she touched, and she submitted willingly to it, knowing that it wasn't meant to conquer her but to join them together.

His hands slid down her back, kneading the soft skin, and everywhere he touched she came alive again. "No more," she whispered frantically. "We're starting all over. I can't take this. I won't be able to say no this time, Kyle."

"Shh..." he put the tip of his roughly callused finger against the smoothness of her lips. "Yes, we're starting all over, but this time you can take what I offer. You don't have to say no."

"You've never understood." She tried to pull away.

"I understand."

"I love you, Kyle. This isn't fair to me."

"I love you, Angelle."

She tried to pull away, frantic to escape. "I love you and I can't keep saying no to y—" Then she stopped, her mouth dropping open. "What did you say?"

"I said—" his voice cracked and he cleared his throat "—I love you, Angelle. I want you to marry me, be a mother to my children, share my home—or your home—" he amended.

"Pardon me," she interrupted, "but are you serious?"

Her incredulity startled him, and he began to shake with laughter, tightening his arms around her so that she could feel the vibrations against her breasts. "Absolutely, soul-crushingly serious. I just don't know why you didn't point out how I was feeling before. It would have saved us a lot of misery."

"Point out your feelings? Are you kidding? I didn't even know you had feelings, you big oaf." She tried to wrestle out of his arms, but he held her in a bear hug until she stopped struggling.

"Now is that any way to talk to your soon-to-be-husband? You're going to have to think of something else to call me. 'You big oaf' isn't dignified, little lady."

She took a deep breath and the smile that resulted when she had completed exhaling was big enough to make her mouth ache. "I'll trade you 'little lady' for 'you big oaf,'" she suggested in a spirit of compromise. "I'm easy."

"No, you aren't. You're the most difficult woman I've ever met. Stubborn, set in your ways, self-righteous, unpredictable, but I'm absolutely, one hundred percent nuts about you."

"And you're rude, overbearing and insensitive, but somehow I love you enough to want to explode from it." She lay back in his arms, letting the tide of warmth sweep over both of them. Sensation returned to flesh that had become numb with hurt and rejection. Like blood coming back into a temporarily sleeping limb, she was alive with feeling, and it was a feeling that was like nothing she had ever experienced.

Finally when he had led her unresisting body to the brink of a passionate new world that she had given up hoping for, he put his hands on her shoulders and pushed her against the back of the couch. With fingers that she could feel trembling through the soft cotton of her sweater, he massaged the tensed muscles of her shoulders and whispered the words she had known he would never say.

"Why did you stop?" she asked finally, when she could control her breathing enough to talk.

"This is going too fast," he said, his voice husky. "Just like everything has from the beginning. It wouldn't be right for you if we continued at this speed."

"Don't be too sure of that," she said, her blue eyes heavy lidded and her lips dewy from the kisses they had shared. "I was keeping up pretty well."

He grinned and pulled her to rest against his chest. Cheek against hard, hair-roughened muscle, she groaned with pleasure. "Tell me when you decided that you loved me," she said, needing to hear it, needing to take her mind off his lovemaking or go crazy with desire.

"I only realized the truth today, but I think I've loved you for a long time."

"What made you realize the truth?" She stroked the curling auburn hair near her cheek and smiled in delight at the shudder that ran through his body.

"For the first time I understood how my father must have felt when he lost my mother. When I watched you walking away, I felt like I had died too. I'd never felt that way before, not ever."

"You were so sure you would never fall in love."

"And I made sure I lived my life in such a way that it could never happen. I'm ashamed to say that I even married a woman that I could never love and who didn't love me. All to keep myself safe from the kind of emotion I was so afraid of."

His fingers were tangled in her hair, and he smoothed it back to kiss her forehead. "And when I felt you moving into my life, I was furious."

"Well, I was furious too," she admitted. "I didn't want you any more than you wanted me."

"All that fury should have been a clue." For a minute they were silent again, lost in each other.

"For me, the first real inkling of what you had come to mean to me came the night of my party," Kyle said pulling reluctantly away. "When I realized that I was feeling jealousy, I just couldn't believe it. Then when I tried to push you into making love to me... I'll always be ashamed of that, Angel. I've never in my life pushed a woman like that.''

"I doubt that you've ever needed to," she said, teasing his chin with her tongue. "And I didn't want you to stop that night, even though I knew it was wrong for us."

"I was frantic to keep you but not smart enough to know why."

"Do you suppose it's possible for two people who have had to conquer so many internal obstacles to live happily ever after?''

"Well," he said, drawing on what they had learned in the adoption home-study group. "My 'parent' says that a blissfully happy marriage is definitely possible. My 'child' says I'll wither away if I don't make the attempt, and my 'adult' says that after taking all facts into consideration, we are darned near perfect for each other.''

"The little lady and the big oaf," she teased.

"Angel and the Saint." He stroked her hair. "You can teach me about my gentler side, and I can teach you how to throw a football.''

"Actually," she said, "my brothers have already taken care of that. I play a darned good game of touch football. You and Young Ki and Jin Ah and I will dig up the turf at Audubon Park.''

"Young Ki and Jin Ah... Now they'll have two parents apiece.''

Angelle pulled away to see his face better. "Oh, no."

Kyle frowned. "What's wrong?''

"The agency has all kinds of rules about how long you have to have been married to adopt a child. They probably won't let us go through with it now."

Kyle smoothed away the anxious lines on her forehead. "Not to worry. Mrs. Simpson gave me her blessing on the phone about two hours ago.''

"You told her before you asked me?''

His answer was a resounding kiss. "I just wanted to be sure that all contingencies were worked out. I didn't want you to worry about anything."

"You still want to go through with the adoption, don't you?" she asked, just to be sure. "I suspect we'll be giving birth to a child or two ourselves."

"Of course I want to go ahead. Young Ki and Jin Ah couldn't be any more wanted than they are."

She relaxed against him again. "My feelings exactly. Tell me, what did Mrs. Simpson say?"

"She said that she was glad to see that we were as intelligent and mature as she had originally thought we were. And she added that if we hadn't finally realized what was going on, she was going to suggest that we both take the decision-making course that ECS offers. According to Mrs. Simpson, she has known for some time that we would end up this way."

"I feel pretty stupid."

"I feel pretty lucky."

"I feel like ending this discussion." Angelle slipped her hands around Kyle's neck and her gaze was steady on his. "There's nothing between us now, Kyle. Nothing that can stop us from loving each other." She pulled his mouth to hers. "Show me you love me, Kyle."

And he did, with patience and with passion he showed her just how much she had come to mean to him. "Angel," he said later, his voice filled with regretful resolve, "this is as far as we're going tonight or any night until we're married."

Her answer was a moan and finally, "Why?"

"Because there's been too much wavering, too many feelings withheld for too long. I don't think you'll feel that I've really committed myself to you until my wedding band is on your finger."

She tried to protest, but he hushed her with his mouth on hers. "I want you to know that when I finally make love to you on our wedding night, what we do is an expression of what I feel for you. I want you completely relaxed and sure of me."

It was a beautifully old-fashioned sentiment, and Kyle's avowal of it made tears run down her cheeks. "And, Angel," he said, kissing away the tears, "no matter what else is modern and liberated about you, I think that on this one thing, we'll go along with old-fashioned feelings."

She hugged him so hard that they almost became one. Kyle was giving her a perfect gift, a gift of unselfish concern. No matter what he wanted, and wanted desperately, he was thinking of her.

"You know," she said after a few minutes as she thoughtfully nibbled his earlobe, "wanting to wait, just to make me more secure, is almost enough in itself."

They both laughed softly, hugging each other even harder. "Don't tempt me, Angel. My self-control only extends so far."

"How far does it extend?" she asked wickedly. "I'd like to know what your limits are."

"I'd say it measures to Saturday."

"A curious unit of measure."

"No, a lovely day for a wedding." Firmly he pushed her off his lap and then, with a gleam in his eye, carefully straightened the soft white dress, lingering on certain pleats and folds until she was giddy with excitement.

"Saturday?" she said when thought returned and they were walking toward his kitchen.

"Yes. Do you mind a simple wedding?"

"It would be the first simple thing about our relationship."

"Everything will be simple now. We'll get married and I'll love you forever. Nothing complicated at all."

"I can't wait."

They passed through Kyle's bedroom, skirting the side of the gigantic bed, and hurried, breaths held, to the kitchen. Safely there, they glanced at each other and burst into laughter. Angelle's face was bright pink as she gasped, "It's no wonder there are so many big families in New Orleans. Every time you want to go anywhere in one of these crazy houses, you have to pass through the bedroom."

"I don't intend to do much passing through, Angel mine." Kyle gathered her to him for a kiss that told her in no uncertain terms how glad he would be when Saturday came.

"So we'll end up with a big family too," she whispered when she could.

As if to be sure they didn't start on it too soon, Kyle opened the back door and pulled her onto the porch where they were instantly surrounded by wagging tails and fluffy purring fur.

"We'll have to remodel the house to accommodate more children," Kyle said, holding her close against the night air. "Tear down the walls between the two sides, add a second story to the back."

"That sounds like what's happened to us. We've torn down our personal walls, and soon we'll be expanding to include a family." She snuggled as close as she could, her softness fitting perfectly against the hard strength of his body. "We'll still have some adjustments to make."

"My dogs and your cat."

"My flowers and your corduroy.

"My love and your love." His lips stroked hers gently. "That's one adjustment that's going to be a pleasure."

The sky was clear with only the liquid light of a crescent moon, and wrapped in each other's arms, they stood for long moments watching it. "That same moon shines down on our children," Angelle said.

"May we make their lives as happy as I feel at this moment."

"And may we remember that the best gift we can give them is a mother and father who are united in love," she added.

"I think," Kyle said, his voice husky with emotion, "that no matter what else is difficult, that part will be easy."

And just to be sure, they spent a few practice minutes, united in love, as two dogs and one cat romped at their feet.

Epilogue

Angelle woke up to an onslaught of sensation. In the distance she could hear the steady pounding of hammers and occasionally, men's voices shouting above the din. Mingled in the air she breathed appreciatively was the smell of pine boughs and freshly brewed coffee. But the best sensation of all came when her fingers contacted warm, velvety skin and hard muscle. Opening her eyes, she saw the man she loved propped on his elbows watching her wake up.

"Kyle," she said with a smile.

"You seem surprised. Who else did you expect?"

"I expected nobody. Sometimes I wake up and I forget for a minute just how much my life has changed."

"Tell me, when you finally realize that you're an old married lady, how do you feel then?"

"Gloriously happy." She put her arms around his neck as they shared a good-morning kiss that threatened to last until noon. "You're almost dressed," she said with a hint of petulance, taking in his dark dress pants and unbuttoned blue shirt.

He laughed at her disappointment, kissing the tip of her nose before pushing away to sit on the edge of the bed. "I wish I had time to oblige you, Angel, but for once, there are other matters that have to take priority."

"What could be more important?" Her eyes widened and she sat up in bed, careless of her state of near undress. "Oh...oh... Now I really am awake. Did the call come?"

"You slept right through the phone call you've been waiting for for months. Ecumenical Children's Services got a cable early this morning from Mrs. Simpson. She and the children are scheduled to arrive in New York at eight-thirty Eastern Standard Time. They'll be here about noon, if all goes well."

Angelle leaped across the bed and threw herself into his arms. "Finally. I can't believe it!"

For a moment, Kyle allowed himself the pleasure of running his fingers down the silky skin of her bare back. "You know, Angel, if you throw yourself at me like that, we might be late for the plane."

But they both knew he was teasing. After months of turmoil, paperwork and just plain fidgeting, they were going to have their children with them at last. Angelle straightened up and gave him a resounding kiss. "What time is it?"

"It's late. My men have been here for an hour tearing the house down, and you didn't even hear them."

She slid off his lap, grabbed a robe that had ended up on the floor in a heap the night before and pulled it on. "Well, if you just didn't keep me awake at night so much."

"Who keeps who awake? It seems to me that last night—"

She put her finger on his lips. "It's all right. I forgive you."

"You're blushing. We've been married for two and a half months and you still blush." He gathered her close. "Before our life changes completely, Angel, I just wanted to tell you something important."

She raised her eyes to his, running her fingers over his eyebrows. "Yes?"

"That—" he bent so that his lips were close to her ear "—that since we've been married, you haven't been a little lady at all."

"Beast!" she said with a laugh, caressing his shin with her toes.

"I love you," he said. "Now go shower. I want to get to the airport as soon as possible, just in case a miracle occurs and the plane is early."

Like an expectant couple who pack an overnight bag two weeks early for the trip to the hospital, Kyle and Angelle had loaded the Volvo with every possible emergency item a three-and five-year-old might need on a twenty-minute trip from the airport. There were blankets, crackers and cans of juice. There were a few simple toys and the appropriate car seat for Jin Ah, or Jennifer, as they were going to call her, having tried to choose a name as close to her Korean one as possible.

Standing at the car door, Angelle looked back at the little shotgun, which didn't look little at all anymore. On the roof were two of Kyle's men, beginning to frame the addition that would run the entire width and half the length of the house. Almost all the interior walls had been demolished and remodeled, making a large living room, a kitchen and dining room, a bedroom for Kyle and Angelle out of the path of traffic, and a temporary bedroom for the children, which would eventually be converted to play space when the addition was completed.

On the door of the house was a four-foot pine wreath dotted with shiny red Christmas ornaments. In the front windows were fat red candles surrounded by holly.

"Have the neighbors complained about the Christmas decorations?" Kyle asked as they pulled away.

"Not a one. I explained that we wanted the kids to have Christmas with us."

"It's late January. Some people have already started decorating for Mardi Gras."

"This is New Orleans. No one cares."

"It's just a good thing the kids are finally coming. The Christmas tree has lost half its needles."

"Do you think Jin Ah...Jennifer liked the doll I sent with Mrs. Simpson?" Angelle had made the little girl a soft sculpture doll with black yarn and Oriental eyes.

"Of course. I'm sure Young Ki...Keith liked the hat and pocket football game we sent too." Kyle shot a glance at Angelle who was chewing her lip. "Nervous?"

She nodded. "I've never been a mother before."

"You'd never been a wife before, and look how good you are at it."

Marriage was wonderful. Kyle was wonderful. When she needed his reassurance, he always knew what to say. They parked the car, found out what gate the flight would arrive in and hurried to begin the last of a long series of agonizing delays.

At noon the flight from New York arrived with no Mrs. Simpson and no children. A frantic call to ECS proved fruitless. They hadn't heard from Mrs. Simpson.

"Let's have lunch," Kyle suggested.

"I'm not leaving here until I'm carrying a child with me," Angelle said stubbornly.

"You'll need to eat something or you won't be strong enough to lift a flea," Kyle said as he guided her to the coffee shop.

They choked down a sandwich, pausing between halves to call the ECS office again. "They still haven't heard," he told a disappointed Angelle. "Let's finish up and see if the next flight from New York has arrived."

A nasal voice was announcing over the loudspeaker that another New York flight had landed as they reached the appropriate gate. "The chances aren't good that they're on this one either," Kyle cautioned. "Don't get your hopes up."

They stood at the end of the long carpeted corridor watching passengers stream by to greet relatives and friends. Just as they were turning to find their way to another phone booth, Angelle grabbed Kyle's arm. "Look!"

In the distance was the figure of the woman they had come to know so well. In her arms was a tiny child, hardly bigger than a Cabbage Patch doll, and walking beside her was a little boy wearing a black-and-gold hat with New Orleans Saints emblazoned on it. Breaths held, they waited.

"Kyle, Angelle," Mrs. Simpson said, a smile creasing her weathered cheek. "May I present Jin Ah, or Jennifer Sullivan, and Young Ki, or Keith Sullivan." She placed the tiny trembling body of the little girl in Angelle's arms and gave the hand of the little boy into Kyle's keeping. "You're a family now," she said with a catch in her voice. "A family."

Stepping back, Mrs. Simpson watched the young couple she had come to love. They were gazing with speechless reverence at Keith and Jennifer, and their feelings were so apparent that she could almost touch them.

Ah...there were the children. Always the children. And this time she knew that at least two of them were right where they were supposed to be. With a smile and a kiss on each teary cheek, she walked away.

Take 4 Silhouette Special Edition novels
FREE

and preview future books in your home for 15 days!

When you take advantage of this offer, you get 4 Silhouette Special Edition® novels FREE and without obligation. Then you'll also have the opportunity to preview 6 brand-new books —delivered right to your door for a FREE 15-day examination period—as soon as they are published.

When you decide to keep them, you pay just $1.95 each ($2.50 each in Canada) *with no shipping, handling, or other charges of any kind!*

Romance *is* alive, well and flourishing in the moving love stories of Silhouette Special Edition novels. They'll awaken your desires, enliven your senses, and leave you tingling all over with excitement... and the first 4 novels are yours to keep. You can cancel at any time.

As an added bonus, you'll also receive a FREE subscription to the Silhouette Books Newsletter as long as you remain a member. Each issue is filled with news on upcoming books, interviews with your favorite authors, even their favorite recipes.

To get your 4 FREE books, fill out and mail the coupon today!

Silhouette Special Edition®

Silhouette Books, 120 Brighton Rd., P.O. Box 5084, Clifton, NJ 07015-5084

Clip and mail to: Silhouette Books,
120 Brighton Road, P.O. Box 5084, Clifton, NJ 07015-5084 *

YES. Please send me 4 FREE Silhouette Special Edition novels. Unless you hear from me after I receive them, send me 6 new Silhouette Special Edition novels to preview each month. I understand you will bill me just $1.95 each, a total of $11.70 (in Canada, $2.50 each, a total of $15.00), with no shipping, handling, or other charges of any kind. There is no minimum number of books that I must buy, and I can cancel at any time. The first 4 books are mine to keep.

BS18R6

Name _____ (please print)

Address _____ Apt. #

City _____ State/Prov. _____ Zip/Postal Code

* In Canada, mail to: Silhouette Canadian Book Club, 320 Steelcase Rd., E., Markham, Ontario, L3R 2M1, Canada
Terms and prices subject to change.
SILHOUETTE SPECIAL EDITION is a service mark and registered trademark. SE-SUB-1

AMERICAN TRIBUTE

Where a man's dreams count for more than his parentage...

Look for these upcoming titles under the Special Edition American Tribute banner.

LOVE'S HAUNTING REFRAIN
Ada Steward #289–February 1986
For thirty years a deep dark secret kept them apart—King Stockton made his millions while his wife, Amelia, held everything together. Now could they tell their secret, could they admit their love?

THIS LONG WINTER PAST
Jeanne Stephens #295–March 1986
Detective Cody Wakefield checked out Assistant District Attorney Liann McDowell, but only in his leisure time. For it was the danger of Cody's job that caused Liann to shy away.

AM-TRIB-1